Marilyn and Me

Marilyn and Me

Ji-min Lee

Translated from the Korean by
Chi-Young Kim

4th ESTATE • *London*

4th Estate
An imprint of HarperCollins*Publishers*
1 London Bridge Street
London SE1 9GF

www.4thEstate.co.uk

First published in Great Britain in 2019 by 4th Estate

1

A catalogue record for this book is
available from the British Library

ISBN 978-0-00-832231-1 (hardback)
ISBN 978-0-00-832232-8 (trade paperback)

Printed and bound in Great Britain by
CPI Group (UK) Ltd, Croydon

MIX
Paper from
responsible sources
FSC™ C007454

Marketing Department,
Twentieth-Century Fox

To Whom It May Concern:

My name is Herbert W. Green and I am currently stationed in Korea with the 31st Regiment, 7th Infantry Division. I am very homesick; Korea is a terrible place. I do not believe I can effectively convey the sorrow and terror I've seen here. I worry about the children who have lost their parents and their homes; where will they sleep tonight? May the grace of God be with them, though perhaps God's blessings are avoiding Korea for the time being.

I write to you from a hospital in Pusan. I was mistakenly hit by napalm by allied troops providing air support and lost many of my comrades in a place called Hwachon, just above the 38th Parallel. Hearing the screams of the dying made me want to die, too. Thankfully I got out of there alive and am getting better.

I am lying in bed recuperating, but the days are long and tedious. Would you be able to send me a new poster of the lovely Miss Monroe? All of us, from my fellow soldiers to the Korean errand boy, dearly love Miss Monroe. Her beautiful smile is like the warm sun and her poster by our beds melts away our worries. I don't even go to the USO shows as I vastly prefer looking at a picture of Miss Monroe. A few days ago, all my pictures of Miss Monroe were stolen. I feel like a man stranded in a desert without water. Please consider what I've been through—I hope you'll send me a poster. I heard Miss Monroe is filming a new movie. We would be thrilled if you could also enclose a few pictures. We would love for Miss Monroe to visit us here, but we know that is a long shot.

I trust that you will grant us our request. Thank you in advance. I wish you all the best.

P.S. If you see Miss Monroe please tell her that we are all rooting for her to be happy.

A Day in the Life of Miss Alice of Seoul

February 12, 1954

I GO TO WORK THINKING OF DEATH.

Hardly anyone in Seoul is happy during the morning commute, but I'm certain I'm one of the most miserable. Once again, I spent all last night grappling with horrible memories—memories of death. I fought them like a girl safeguarding her purity, but it was no use. I knew I was under an old cotton blanket but I tussled with it as if it were a man or a coffin lid or heavy mounds of dirt, trusting that night would eventually end and death couldn't be this awful. Finally, morning dawned. I looked worn out but tenacious, like a stocking hanging from my vanity. I used a liberal amount of Coty powder on my face to scare the darkness away. I put on my stockings, my dress, and my black, fingerless lace gloves. I walk down the early morning streets as the vicious February wind whips my calves. I can't possibly look pretty, caked as I am in makeup and shivering in the cold. Enduring would be a more apt description. *Those who endure have a chance at beauty.* I read that sentence once in some book. I've been testing that theory for the last few years, although my doubts are mounting.

As always, the passengers in the streetcar glance at me, unsettled. I am Alice J. Kim—my prematurely gray hair is dyed with beer and under a purple dotted scarf, I'm wearing a black wool coat and scuffed dark blue velvet shoes, and my lace gloves are as unapproachable as a widow's black veil at a funeral. I look like a doll discarded by a bored foreign girl. I don't belong in this city, where the ceasefire was declared not so long ago, but at the same time I might be the most appropriate person for this place.

I get off the streetcar and walk briskly. The road to the US military base isn't one for a peaceful, leisurely stroll. White steam plumes up beyond the squelching muddy road. Women are doing laundry for the base in oil drums cut in half, swallowing hot steam as though they are working in hell. I avoid the eyes of the begging orphans wearing discarded military uniforms they've shortened themselves. The abject hunger in their bright eyes makes my gut clench. I shove past the shoeshine boys who tease me, thinking I'm a working girl who services foreigners, and hurry into the base. Snow remaining on the rounded tin roof sparkles white under the clear morning sun. Warmth rolls over me as soon as I open the office door. This place is unimaginably peaceful, so different from the outside world. My black Underwood typewriter waits primly on my desk. I first put water in the coffee pot—the cup of coffee I have first thing when I get in is my breakfast. I can't discount the possibility that I work at the military base solely for the free coffee. I see new documents I'll have to translate into English and into Korean. These are simple, not very important matters that can be handled by my English skills. First, I have to notify the Korean public security bureau that the US military will be participating in the Arbor Day events. Then I have to compose in English the plans for the baseball game between the two countries to celebrate the American Independence Day. My work basically consists of compiling useless information for the sake of binational amity.

"It's freezing today, Alice," Hammett says as he walks into the office, smiling his customary bright smile. "Seoul is as cold as Alaska."

"Alaska? Have you been?" I respond, not looking up from the typewriter.

"Haven't I told you? Before heading to Camp Drake in Tokyo, I spent some time at a small outpost in Alaska called Cold Bay. It's frigid and barren. Just like Seoul."

"I'd like to visit sometime." I try to imagine a part of the world that is as discarded and ignored as Seoul, but I can't.

"I have big news!" Hammett changes the subject, slamming his hand on my desk excitedly.

I've never seen him like this. Startled, my finger presses down on the Y key, making a small bird footprint on the paper.

"You heard Marilyn Monroe married Joe DiMaggio, right? They're on their honeymoon in Japan. Guess what—they're coming here! It's nearly finalized. General Christenberry asked her to perform for the troops and she immediately said yes. Can you believe it?"

Marilyn Monroe. She moves like a mermaid taking her precarious first steps, smiling stupidly, across the big screen rippling with light.

Hammett seems disappointed at my tepid response to this thrilling news. To him, it might be more exciting than the end of the Second World War.

"She's married?" I say.

"Yes, to Joe DiMaggio. Two American icons in the same household! This is a big deal, Alice!"

I vaguely recall reading about Joe DiMaggio in a magazine. A famous baseball player. To me, Marilyn Monroe seems at odds with the institution of marriage.

"Even better," Hammett continues, "they are looking for a female soldier to accompany her as her interpreter. I recommended you! You're not a soldier, of course, but you have experience. You'll spend four days with her as the Information Service representative. Isn't that exciting? Maybe I should follow her around. Like Elliott Reid in *Gentlemen Prefer Blondes*."

Why is she coming to this godforsaken land? After all, American soldiers thank their lucky stars that they weren't born Korean.

"We have a lot to do—we have to talk to the band, prepare a bouquet, and get her a few presents. What do you think we should give her? Folk crafts aren't that special. Oh, what if you draw a portrait of her? Stars like that sort of thing."

"A portrait?" I stammer, flushing all the way down my neck. "You can ask the PX portrait department—"

Hammett grins mischievously. "You're the best artist I know."

My mouth is dry. "I—I haven't drawn anything in a long time." I am as ashamed as an unmarried girl confessing she is pregnant. "And—and—I don't know very much about her."

"There's nothing easier! People with faces that are easy to draw are the ones who become stars anyway. You don't have to know anything about her. She is what you see." He's having a ball but then sobers when he catches my eye. That sharp gaze behind his good-natured laughter confirms the open secret that he probably is an intelligence officer. "Why don't you draw anymore, anyway? You were a serious artist."

I'm flustered and trapped, and my fingers slip. Letters scatter across the white paper like broken branches. He might be the only one who remembers the person I was during more illustrious times. Among the living, that is. "No, no. If I were a true artist I would have died in the war," I murmur, and pretend to take a sip of coffee. My words leap into my coffee like a girl committing suicide. The resulting black ripples reverberate deep into my heart.

* * *

I leave work earlier than usual and take the streetcar to Namdaemun Gate.

A few months before the war broke out, a thoughtful someone had hung a Korean flag, an American flag, and a sign that exclaimed, "WELCOME US NAVY!" from the top of the centuries-old fortress gate. Perhaps thanks to its unceasing support of the US military, Namdaemun survived, though it suffered grievous wounds. I look at the landmark, the nation's most famous disabled veteran, unable to offer any reassuring words. As if confused about how it survived, Namdaemun sits abjectly and seems to convey it would rather part ways with Seoul. I express my keen agreement as I pass it by.

The entrance to Chayu Market near Namdaemun teems with pedestrians, merchants, and American soldiers. All manner of dialects mingle with the pleasant Seoul accent and American slang. I fold my shoulders inward and try not to bump into anyone. The vitality and noise pumping out of the market are as intense and frightening as those on a battlefield. I am unable to keep up with the hunger for survival the people around me exude, so I make sure to stay out of their way. I duck around a fedora-wearing gentleman holding documents under his arm, a woman with a child on her back with an even larger bundle balanced on her head, and a man performing the acrobatic trick of napping on his feet, leaning against his A-frame. I head further into the market.

At Mode Western Boutique, I find a group of women from the market who are part of an informal credit association. Mrs. Chang, who owns the boarding house I live in, also owns the boutique and oversees the group. The women are trading gossip over bolts of shiny Chinese silk and velour, but when I walk in they poke at each other, clamming up instantly. I'm used to their curious but scornful glances. I pretend not to notice and shoot Mrs. Chang a look in lieu of a greeting. Mrs. Chang swiftly collects the bills spread out on her purple brocade skirt and stands up.

"Ladies, you know Miss Kim, one of my boarders? She's a typist at the base. Don't you embarrass yourselves by saying anything in English."

The women begin exchanging smutty jokes and laughing. With the women otherwise occupied, Mrs. Chang ushers me into the small room at the back of the shop. She turns on the light, revealing the English labels on dizzying stacks of cans, cigarettes, and makeup smuggled out of the base.

"Here you go." I take out the dirty magazine I wrapped in pages torn out of a calendar. I asked an accommodating houseboy to get me a copy.

Mrs. Chang glances outside and gestures at me to lower my voice. She flips through the magazine rapidly and frowns upon seeing a white girl's breasts, as large as big bowls. "Even these rags are better when they're American-made," she says, smiling awkwardly. "A good customer has been looking for this. I've been searching and searching, but the ones I come across are already fairly used, you know?"

I turn away from Mrs. Chang's feeble excuse.

Mrs. Chang shows these magazines to her impotent husband. She lost all three of her children during the war. That is sad enough, but it's unbearable that she's trying for another child with her husband, who stinks of the herbal medicine he takes for his ailments. It's obscene to picture this middle-aged woman, whose lower belly is now shrunken, opening *Playboy* for her husband who can barely sit up as she pines for her dead children. It's too much to handle for even me.

"I'm sorry I had to ask an innocent girl like you to do an errand like this for me," she says.

"That's all right. Who says I'm innocent?"

Mrs. Chang studies me disapprovingly. "Don't stay out too late. I'll leave your dinner by your door." Although her words are brusque, Mrs. Chang is the one person who worries about whether I'm eating enough.

Having fled the North during the war, Mrs. Chang is famously determined, as is evident in her success. She is known throughout the market for her miserly cold-heartedness. That's how pathetic I am—even someone like her is worried about me.

We met at the Koje Island refugee camp. In her eyes, I'm still hungry and traumatized. I was untrustworthy and strange back then, shunned even by the refugees. I babbled incoherently, in clear, sophisticated Seoul diction, sometimes even using English. I fainted any time I had to stand in line and shredded my blanket as I wept in the middle of the night. I was known as the crazy rich girl

8

who had studied abroad. I cemented my reputation with a shocking incident and after that Mrs. Chang took it upon herself to monitor me. When she looks at me I feel the urge to show her what people expect from me, though I doubt she wants me to. People seem to think I have lost my will to stand on my own two feet and that I will fall apart dramatically. I'm not being paranoid. I haven't even exited the boutique and the women are already sizing up my bony rump and unleashing negative observations about how hard it would be for me to bear a child. They wouldn't believe it even if I were to lie down in front of them right now and give birth. Somehow I have become a punchline.

Alice J. Kim. People do not like her.

Women approach me with suspicion and men walk away, having misunderstood me. Occasionally someone is intrigued, but they are a precious few; foreigners or those whose kindness is detrimental to their own well-being. People don't approve of me, beginning with my name. "Alice? Are you being snooty because you happen to know a little English?"

Very few know my real name, or why I discarded Kim Ae-sun to become Alice. I'm the one person in the world who knows what my middle initial stands for. Only whores or spies take on an easy-to-pronounce foreign name—I am either disappointing my parents or betraying my country. People think I am a prostitute who services high-level American military officers; at one point I was known as the UN whore, which is certainly more explicit than UN madam. But I was just grateful to be linked to an entity that is working for world peace. Or else they say I'm insane. Now, to be a whore and insane at the same time—if I were a natural phenomenon, I would be that rare unlucky day that brings both lightning and hail. People will occasionally summon their courage to ask me point-blank. Once, an American officer took out his wallet, saying, "I'd like to see for myself. Do an Oriental girl's privates go horizontal or vertical?" I told him, "Every woman's privates look the same as your mother's." The officer cleared his throat in embarrassment before fleeing. Anyway, in my experience, a life shrouded in suspicion isn't always bad. No matter how awful, keeping secrets is more protective than revealing the truth. Secrets tend to draw out the other person's fear. Without secrets, I would be completely destitute.

Once, I heard Mrs. Chang attempt to defend me. "Listen. It wasn't just one or two women who went insane during the war. We all saw mothers trying to breastfeed their dead babies and maimed little girls crawling around looking for their younger siblings. I remember an old woman in Hungnam who embraced her disabled son while they leaped off the wharf to their deaths." She implied that I was just one of countless women who had gone crazy during the war, and that I should be accepted as such. But even Mrs. Chang, who considers herself my guardian, most certainly doesn't like me. I've been brought into her care because the intended recipients of her maternal instinct have died. Maternal instinct—I've never had it, but I wonder if it's similar to opium. You can try to stay away from it your entire life, but it would be incredibly hard to quit if you've tasted it. That is what maternal instinct is—grand and powerful and far-reaching. During the war the most heartbreaking scenes were of mothers standing next to their dead children. Maybe not. The most heartbreaking scenes during the war can't be described in words.

In any case, perhaps confusing me for her daughter, Mrs. Chang meddles constantly in my affairs. It goes without saying that she has a litany of complaints. She looks at me with contempt. After all, I rinse my hair with beer, a tip I learned from an actual prostitute. That is certainly something to look down on, but I do have my reasons. My hair is completely gray. One autumn long ago, I grew old in the span of a single day. Afterward my hair never returned to its true color. My unsightly hair has the texture of rusted rope, but I'm satisfied with it for the time being. Mrs. Chang also despises my vulgar clothes, unbefitting, she says, of my status as an educated woman. But none of the things I'd learned academically helped me in the decisive moment of my life; my intelligence and talents, though not that deep or superior, were actually what entrapped me. Nor does Mrs. Chang think highly of my personality. She says I am haughty, which she thinks is why I don't like people, but she's not entirely correct. The truth is that I'm too broken. In any case, she cares for me in her heartless way and keeps me near. Even stranger is that I can't seem to leave her, though I too look down on her. Our unusual connection yokes us together despite everything. She probably feels the sharp wind of Hungnam when she sees my bloodless cheeks. My pale forehead would remind her of the Koje Island refugee camp, where we were doused with anti-lice DDT powder as we sat on the dirt floor. Though we never meant to, we have somehow lived our lives together. We have a special bond, like all those who experienced war. We shared times of life and death. And she clearly remembers my triumphs and my defeats.

I triumphed by surviving but ended up surrendering; I tried to hang myself in the refugee camp, an act so shocking it cemented my reputation as a crazy woman. Mrs. Chang happened to walk by and pulled me down with her strong arms and brought me back to my senses with her vulgar cursing. Why did I want to plunge into death after I'd survived bombings and massacres? I still don't understand my reasons, but Mrs. Chang is certain in her own conjectures and stays by my side to watch over me. Hers is not the gaze of an older woman looking compassionately at a younger one. It's the sad ache of a woman who is well-versed in misfortune, feeling sympathy for a woman who is still uncomfortable with tragedy. If there's a truth I've learned over the last few years, it's that a woman's strength comes not from age but from misfortune. I want to be exempted from this truth. I have earned the right to be strong but now I do not want this strength. A woman becomes lonely the moment she realizes her strength. As loneliness is altogether too banal, for the moment I would like to politely decline.

I leave Chayu Market and head towards Myong-dong.

Wind enters through my parted lips, cold enough to form a layer of thin ice on my tongue. I swirl my tongue around and swallow it. Having passed through the desolate city, the wind has an odd candy sweetness to it. Not many people are out on the street and for that I am grateful.

A streetcar crammed with people pulls up as I stand at the traffic circle in front of Bank of Korea. Teeming with black heads, the car resembles a lunch box filled with black beans cooked in soy sauce. Everyone is expressionless, making me wonder why we even have eyes, noses, or mouths. I stare at those stone-faced people and gradually their features begin to disappear, leaving behind only their black hair. I can't breathe. I feel dizzy. I close my eyes and turn away. The streetcar continues down the street and I let out a sigh, as though freed from a corset. I look around to see if anyone has seen my reaction. There is no cure for this. Even after all this time, I have a physical reaction in a mass of people. It harms my dignity; shuddering like a pissing dog every time I find myself in the middle of a crowd doesn't fit the independent life I seek. People who'd witnessed my reaction spread the rumor that I had gone insane. They might expect that I would make profuse apologies but I refuse to do so.

I walk past the Central Post Office and spot a hunchback child sitting out front. Wrapped in a ragged blanket and wearing a newspaper-thin skirt, she is begging. She scratches a spoon on an empty brass bowl and emits a sound more desperate than the Lord's Prayer. Could that child become a woman without being violated? That's what I worry about. I turn away, unable to meet her gaze. I hear a baby's cry. My head snaps around. The girl's rounded spine straightens and a head pops up. She had her infant sibling on her back all along. The baby wails, arching its neck, and the girl looks up at the sky and mumbles, too weak to soothe it. Her dark eyes reflect nothing. She may never have even heard of such unrealistic concepts as hopes or dreams. I rummage through my bag and find a broken Hershey's bar. I toss it at the girl and rush off. The chocolate won't solve the child's hunger; it'll just introduce her to the easy temptation of sweetness. Unable to forget that chocolaty taste, she will continue on the streets. That is the purpose of a Hershey's bar, which befriends both soldiers and children during war.

"Did you read *Mrs. Freedom* yesterday?" Yu-ja asks, heating steel chopsticks in the flame of the stove. "What do you think will happen next? Don't you think Professor Chang's wife will sleep with her next-door neighbor? I'm positive she will. Isn't the very term 'next-door neighbor' so seductive? I'd say it straddles the line between melodrama and erotica."

Yu-ja works as a receptionist at Myong-dong Clinic, which is set back from the bustling main thoroughfare. That may be why it's never too busy when I stop by to see her. It's a dull place for a vivacious girl like Yu-ja, who seems always to be moving to the music of a dance hall band.

"That's all anyone talks about these days," I say. "As if they don't know how contradictory the two words are together—Mrs. and Freedom."

Seoul Sinmun, which is publishing *Mrs. Freedom* as a serial, is open on Yu-ja's desk. It's the talk of the town. Yu-ja reads each installment passionately. In fact, she rereads it several times a day.

"That old-maid intellectual sarcasm of yours! You know men hate that, right?" Yu-ja counts slowly to twenty, twirling her bangs around the heated chopstick. When she takes the chopstick out, her hair emerges not as Jean Harlow's Hollywood wave but as a sad, limp curl like a strand of partially rehydrated seaweed. To make up for her failed attempt at a wave, Yu-ja pats another layer of Coty powder on her face. She tugs on a new skirt, struggling on the examination table. She's quite alluring. When I look at her round, peach-like face, I can't believe she signed up to be a cadet nurse in the war.

In order to secure a place on an evacuation train during the Third Battle of Seoul, Yu-ja had run to the recruiting district headquarters inside the Tonhwamun Gate at Changdokgung Palace, having seen a recruitment ad for nurse officers in the paper. She was ordered to assemble at

Yongdungpo Station that same day, and she dashed across the frozen Han River just as the last train evacuating the war wounded was about to leave. As soon as she boarded, Yu-ja was tasked with helping soldiers to go to the bathroom and spent the next few days working incessantly on that train, which traveled only at night. One early morning, as the train pulled into some countryside station, Yu-ja was using the dawn light coming through the window to search for and eat the bits of rice the patients had dropped, and in that moment she truly knew despair. Once in Pusan, Yu-ja put on a US Army work uniform and even went through basic training, but, worried about her family, gave up her dream of becoming a cadet nurse. Yu-ja experienced her own hardships during those years; not until fairly recently has she been able to powder her face so liberally. I understand why she's rushing around with her womanhood in full bloom. A flower's lifespan is ten days but a woman's spring is even shorter. Many a spring died during the war. The mere fact that she survived has given Yu-ja the right to bloom fully.

"Are you going back to the officers' club tonight? Your dance steps aren't up to standard," I tease.

Yu-ja smiles confidently. "You're going to want to buy me a beer when you hear what I have to tell you. Ready for this? Remember I told you that one of our patients is married to the chairman of the Taegu School Foundation? Her family operates several orphanages and daycare centers. I mentioned Chong-nim and she said she would ask around. I think she has some news for us!"

Chong-nim. My mouth falls open and my breathing grows shallow.

"Go ahead and close your mouth," Yu-ja says teasingly. "How *do* you earn a living when you act like this?" Yu-ja is hard on me and at the same time worries about me. I wouldn't let anyone else do that but I humbly allow her. Mrs. Chang saved me from death while Yu-ja took me in when I went crazy. All of that happened in Pusan—goddamn Pusan, that hellish temporary wartime capital of South Korea. Each time Yongdo Bridge drew open, stabbing at the sky like the gates to hell, I believed that an enraged Earth had finally churned itself upside down to proclaim complete disaster. The streets were lined with shacks built out of ration boxes and the smell of burning fuel mixed with the stench of shit. I spent days lying like a corpse in a tiny room as rain dripped through the roof reinforced with military-issue raincoats. I want to eat Japanese buckwheat noodles, I told anyone who would listen. Yu-ja would empty my chamber pot when she got home from work and snap, Please get a grip on yourself. Why are you acting like this? Why? I could understand Yu-ja's frustration. To her, it was unimaginable that I could have a tragic future. I knew Yu-ja, who was a few years younger, from the church I attended for a bit after liberation. We were never close but she always showed an interest in me. When I was transported to a hospital in Pusan, Yu-ja was working there as a nursing assistant. I didn't recognize her; I was at my worst, unable to utter my own name, but Yu-ja remembered even my most

17

trivial habits. I had been the object of envy to young Yu-ja, having studied art in Ueno, Tokyo, and worked for the American military government. She remembered me as quite the mysterious and alluring role model. It might have been because I was harboring the most daring yet ordinary secret a young woman could have—being in love with a married man. That was a long time ago, when I was still called Kim Ae-sun.

And now she is talking about Chong-nim. Her name makes me alert. I've been looking for that girl for the last three years, that child with whom I don't share even a drop of blood, the five-year-old who grabbed my hand trustingly as we escaped Hungnam amid ten thousand screaming refugees, where we would have died if we hadn't managed to slip onto the ship. If I were to write about my escape I would dedicate the story to her. To the girl who would be nine by now, her nose cute and flat and her teeth bucked, from Huichon of Chagang Province. Her hopes were small and hot, like the still-beating heart of a bird. Her will to survive roused me from Hungnam and miraculously got us on the *Ocean Odyssey* headed to Pusan. It was December 24, 1950. The night of Christmas Eve was more miraculous and longer than any night in Bethlehem. I wouldn't have lost her if I hadn't acted like a stupid idiot. She disappeared as I lay in the refugee camp infirmary, conversing with ghosts. She became one of many war orphans, their bellies distended and their hair cut short, buried in the heartless world.

"The orphanage is somewhere in Pohang," continues Yu-ja. "There's a nine-year-old girl, and she came from Hungnam around the time you did. I heard she has the watch you talked about. What other orphan would own an engraved Citizen pocket watch?"

My—no, his—watch that I gave to her, which she tucked in the innermost pocket of her clothes. It had been our only keepsake. That small watch is probably ticking away with difficulty just like me, cherishing time that can't be turned back.

"Where is it? Where do we need to go?" I spring to my feet.

Yu-ja tries to calm me down. "I don't know all the details. I'm supposed to meet her this evening at the dance hall. Why don't you come with me? There are too many orphans, and the records are so spotty it's hard to find them. The lady managed to get in touch with a nun who saw a girl that fits her description somewhere in Pohang."

But Yu-ja is unable to convince me to wait and has to run after me without putting the finishing touches to her makeup. Next to fresh, fashionable Yu-ja I look even more grotesque. Yu-ja is a young female cat who's just learned to twirl her tail, and I'm an old, molting feline who can barely remember the last time she was in heat. I'm not yet thirty but I feel like an old hag who has forgotten everything.

We go down the stairs. Yu-ja tugs my arm at the entrance to the obstetrics clinic; a young girl is squatting in the cold hallway, wearing a quilted skirt, a man's maroon sweater, and a black woolen scarf wound around her face. Her gaze is feral, sad, and cold, a dizzy tangle of defensiveness and aggression. Yu-ja pulls me along. "She's a maid for some rich family in Namsan," she whispers. "Did you hear what happened? The master of the house raped her and now she's pregnant. Then he and his wife accused her of seducing him, beat her, and threw her out. Apparently she has eight younger siblings back home. She was here yesterday too, asking for help to get rid of it. So many maids are in her situation. I feel bad for them. They try to get rid of it by taking quinine pills—it's so dangerous."

We step into the street and the wind delivers a hard slap. The maid's rage and despair scatter in the wind. This city poisons girls and women, young and old. Girls with tragic fates are merely a small segment of the people who make up the city. The light they emit in order to hide their shame turns the city even more dazzling at night. The streetlights go on and the light seeps into my heart. It has taken in yet another unforgettable gaze.

It's still early but the dance hall is crowded.

The dancers are gyrating enthusiastically, as though it's the last dance of the night. This is a sacred place for the wild women of these postwar times, these women who rightfully intimidate men. Of course, men dance too, but women own this place. A rainbow of velour skirts and nylon dresses twirl like flower petals. There are café madams, owners of downtown boutiques, restaurateurs, dollar exchangers, rich war widows, wives of high-level officials, teachers, concubines, college students—I am taken aback that these are all women who have lived through the war. Maybe they hung their grief and pain on the heavy, sparkling chandelier. I'm jealous of these women whose desire to dance is so intense, who look as if they would keep dancing no matter what. Having learned the futility of life, they move lightly without any regrets. I can't do that. My breath catches in my throat as I watch them dance, skin to skin. The sight calls to mind images of the masses, moving with a single purpose. As I stand there, dazed, Yu-ja pushes me towards a table in the middle of the room. The chairman's wife and the wives of business and political leaders, all in fox stoles, greet us.

"I understand you're fluent in English and you studied in Tokyo," the chairman's wife says. "My son is preparing to study in America. I would ask you to tutor him if you weren't a woman." She laughs. The other wives look askance at my whorish hair and my tattered black lace gloves. By the time their eyes settle on my worn stockings, they are concluding I am not who I purport to be.

I cut to the chase. "When can I see Chong-nim?"

The chairman's wife gestures at me to be patient and pours me a beer. "The nun I met at the single mothers' home told me about a girl who fits that description. Something about a pocket watch? I put in a special request to find her. You can go to this address and ask for Sister Chong Sophia." She smiles as she hands me a card.

I bow in gratitude. She takes my hand. She's drunk. Her eyes betray a hollow elegance unique to a woman of leisure.

Meanwhile, Yu-ja is craning to find someone. "Look who's here!" she says, clapping and springing to her feet.

The band is now playing a waltz. Perfume ripples and crests against the wall. Beyond the couples moving off the dance floor is Park Ku-yong, who scans the room until he spots Yu-ja. He waves and comes towards us. Alarmed, I try to duck under the table as Yu-ja grabs me and pulls me up. Ku-yong is wearing a black, faded university uniform and an embarrassed expression, as if he is fully aware that he doesn't quite belong. His footsteps, however, are as assured as ever, obliterating the rhythm of the waltz as he walks towards us. I glare at Yu-ja and pinch her hand.

At our table, Ku-yong bows and the women welcome the opportunity to tease me. "Oh, you must be Miss Alice's boyfriend!"

Ku-yong smiles in embarrassment. I can't in good conscience make him stand there like this so I quickly say my goodbyes and take my leave. Yu-ja laughs and wishes me luck. She's certain that this man has feelings for me. She might be right, but I haven't confirmed it. I want to avoid the chronic mistake of a lonely woman, confusing a man's kindness for love. Any special feelings he might have for me are more likely sympathy.

"You came all this way but you're not even going to dance?" This is Ku-yong's attempt at a joke, but I look away.

I can't dance with him. You don't dance with a man who regards you with sympathy. You can drink with him and even sleep with him, but you can't dance with him. That would be insulting to the beautiful music and the sparkling chandelier.

Ku-yong and I walk apart from each other like an old-fashioned couple who keep a decorous distance in public.

Worried that his gaze might land on my body somewhere, I shiver for no reason at all. "What are you doing here?"

"I was at Yu-ja's clinic last week with an unwell coworker. She told me I would see you today if I came by. I'm glad I did."

I look down at his shadow stretched out next to me. He's probably not eating well either but his shadow is sturdy. His interior is likely hollow, though. What once filled his soul has probably leaked away. I know because that's what happened to me. We were artists once, but now we barely remember how to hold a pencil. I make a living with my clumsy English skills while he is stuck doing manual labor at the US military ammunition depot in Taepyongno.

The silence makes me uneasy. "Marilyn Monroe is coming to Korea," I blurt out. It's never advantageous to talk about a prettier woman than oneself but I am curious about his reaction.

Ku-yong widens his already big eyes and raises his arms in a silent cheer. That's the power of Marilyn. "Can you believe she's married? You'll have to find someone your-self, don't you think?" He glances at me.

I'm charmed by his effort to link Marilyn's life to mine. I let out a laugh. "Gentlemen prefer blondes, which you know I'm not." No gentleman likes prematurely gray hair washed with beer. But I also can't stand gentlemen. The two men I loved were gentlemen and they both disguised their true selves with well-tailored suits and nice manners. The man who ruins a young lady's reputation is often a gentleman who walks her home at night.

"Alice, have you been drawing?" Ku-yong asks suddenly.

I glance up at him. Mediocre people like us don't dare talk about war or art, the great subjects of humanity. If there is anything we learned, it's that you avoid war and art to the best of your ability if you want to live your life to its natural end. "No. And you?"

"I've started to. On postcards this big." He shows me with his hands. "I draw the stream I can see from my room. I don't have interesting ideas like before; I just draw what I see—reality."

His answer lands like a punch. I was certain he wouldn't be drawing either. I turn to look at him. He rubs his peanut-shaped face with his wool gloves, his white breath hanging in the air. He resembles his own cartoon charac-ter. As I was familiar with his cartoons that ran in news-papers and magazines, I recognized him instantly when I met him for the first time. Ku-yong, who studied art in Japan, wasn't famous, but he enjoyed a quiet fan base of passionately devoted readers—I was one of them. Truth

Seeker, the main character of his editorial cartoons, was a sly and honest thinker, just like him, and Dandy Boy, the main character of the adventure cartoon serialized in a youth magazine, was a stubborn dreamer whose future seemed precarious, just like his. He was the rare artist who loved his work without being taken over by it. It's entirely because of the war that someone like him now does odd jobs wearing cotton work gloves instead of handling sharp pen nibs.

The war broke out during a brutal, broiling summer. Every day until I crawled home, exhausted, in the evening, I was shut inside a small room, drawing dozens of Stalin portraits for the Democratic People's Republic of Korea, while downstairs Ku-yong drew propaganda posters exhorting the North Korean People's Army to launch a full-scale offensive. We were two loyal dogs with a talent for drawing; I was the female on the verge of starving to death, repenting my consorting with American imperialists, and he was the quiet male bringing me balls of rice and water. I didn't feel well and spilled as many tears as I shed drops of sweat. People think Communism was what treated me poorly, but in reality it was myself. I would drink from the cup of water I washed my brushes in as I willed the awful summer to pass. At that point I didn't know the half of it. When the recapture of Seoul by the southern forces was imminent, Ku-yong was taken north before I was, but managed to make a dramatic escape and reach safety. Eventually, the South determined that he had collaborated with the enemy and took him into custody. His talents were highly valued, however, and he was thus assigned to the psychology unit of the army headquarters and began to draw cartoons for the Ministry of National Defense. Whereas he once conveyed the grand news of victory for the People's Army, he now began to depict women being violated by the Chinese Communists in a new, realistic, graphic style, broadcasting the tragedy of war. Ku-yong told me later that he could smell ink even in his sleep; even fermented soybeans would smell like paint. He returned to Seoul after the South retook the capital and decided he was done with art. This decision was as logical as the laws of nature in which spring followed winter. It also revealed his respect towards his newly recovered freedom.

Last year, when I bumped into him in Chong-dong, he explained bluntly why he had stopped drawing: "You see, it's a waste of time for me to sit inside a room all day."

Oddly enough that comment made me feel at ease. At first, even acknowledging his existence reminded me of that demonic summer, which made me want to avoid him, but his loneliness and his reclusive tendencies pulled me in. After all he was a colleague from a wretched phase in our lives. We had both exhausted our God-given talents in this godforsaken land.

"Ae-sun—I mean, Alice—I think I'm going to make art again."

I have nothing to say to that. I should be applauding him for starting over, for overcoming his wounds and his helplessness, but I turn away, my hands laced together. It shouldn't be a surprise to him that I'm this ungenerous; I'm dismayed that my friend is no longer defeated or despairing. I feel instantly alone. I'm disappointed with myself.

"Shall we walk towards Chonggyechon?" he asks. "We can get something to eat on the way."

That's such a long, dirty walk, especially in these worn shoes. But I don't voice my feelings. What made him change his mind? I feel as if I've been punched twice today: Hammett's words to me in the office are still buzzing in my ears and now even Ku-yong is irritating me. I could make excuses and tell myself I wasn't such a great artist anyway, but I'm enveloped by a strange guilt.

We pass Supyo Bridge and the shacks balanced on either side of Chonggyechon. Built from rough pieces of wood, the shacks appear to have been made with the remnants of Noah's Ark. It's as if Noah and his descendants managed to survive by eating the animals they saved. The evening is filled with the smell of food and filth, along with the sounds of clean laundry being ironed, beaten with sticks, and of babies crying. A worker cleaning his tools at a hardware store spots us and smiles slyly. We must look like pathetically destitute lovers out on a date.

Ku-yong takes me to his favorite bar. A *Homecoming* poster is stuck to the greasy wood-paneled wall. Clark Gable's and Lana Turner's nice smiles are incongruous with this place. The barmaid's son, playing marbles in front of the furnace, greets us spiritedly and shows us to a fairly clean table. The barmaid, who was serving liquor up in the loft, quickly slips down the ladder. I must be hungrier than

I realized; before the mungbean pancakes arrive at our table, I empty half a kettle of makgolli. Ku-yong keeps pouring me more. By the time he starts to irritate me, I realize I'm drunk. I loosen my grip on my cup.

"I hope great things happen for you this year," he says, smiling and tearing a piece of pancake for me. Affection lingers in his eyes.

I'm confused. I hope he'll stop at sympathy. Affection disarms you. I don't want any of it. I prefer to be honestly misunderstood than insincerely understood. "You've somehow managed to find hope for yourself so you're all set," I say tartly.

He doesn't deflate. That alone makes me feel trapped. "Ae-sun—I mean, Alice," he begins. I can tell from his voice that he's been considering what to say for a long time. "I hope you'll find peace. I've been living the last few years like an idiot. I don't regret it, of course, but I want to have a different life. I hope you'll be able to forget the past, too. This isn't you. We both know it."

I stare resolutely at the table, refusing to meet his eye.

"Be with me. In whatever way that may be. Ae-sun—I mean, Alice …" Ku-yong isn't even embarrassed. He's as earnest and frank as his cartoon characters.

I must have sensed that something like this would happen. That must be why I came along. I decide to save him by putting a firm end to this ridiculous melodrama. "You can't be with me, Ku-yong. You can't understand my pain. Do you know why? I've killed. I've killed a child. And then I went insane and tried to kill myself. I failed at doing that so I went crazy. I'm fine now, but you never know when I'll lose my mind again."

The boy, who was eavesdropping, scampers off in shock. Ku-yong stares down at the floor uneasily. He doesn't even attempt to take in what I'm saying. "Stop with the bitterness and mockery. That's not you."

For some reason this makes me sad. "Let go of your expectations. Don't waste whatever remaining love you have for humanity on me."

"You're so frustrating, Ae-sun! Look around. People are living, they're being strong, they're as good as new. Why do you keep insisting on staying in the past?"

I lose my confidence for a moment. "Why do you want to take on my nightmares I don't want to remember?" I ask. "What do you know about me, anyway? Do you remember the state I was in when we bumped into each other last year? You looked at me like you'd lost all hope for me."

In fact, Ku-yong regarded me with shock, like a burn victim seeing himself in the mirror for the first time. Anyone else making that expression would have infuriated me, but oddly enough I stared at him with the same expression on my face.

"Don't you remember?" I ask him. "I looked just like Seoul—hopeless, though nobody wanted to say that out loud. I was at my worst in Pusan, but I wasn't much better back here. I tried, though. I tried to be ordinary and be one of those people. But it didn't work for long. One day I was walking downtown and I passed the bombed-out fire station. All the windows were gone and you could see the darkness inside. It was like an enormous skull with two eye sockets. It began to laugh, its jaw juddering. I jumped onto the first streetcar that came. But it started to fill up and I was stuck among people and I couldn't breathe and I was sweating and my ribs felt like they were breaking and I could hear a horrible noise and everything turned dark. I started to smell blood, and every time people brushed against me I felt like I was being torn to pieces. I sank down, below people's legs. I was curled up like that on the floor, screaming for help. Do you know what they did? In order to gawk at me properly, they managed to move around in an orderly way in that over-crowded car. Watching a crazy woman is more entertaining than a fire, isn't it? As soon as I felt people's eyes on me, I turned mute. The heel of my shoe broke off and I was foaming at the mouth and it got all over me and nobody came to help. Finally a woman with a child on her back elbowed her way through from the end and took off the cloth that was holding her child to cover my thighs. Menstrual blood was streaming down them. I saw relief in people's eyes, glad that they weren't me. A few men leered, peering overtly between my legs. I accepted it then, that I always was and still am someone who makes people uncomfortable. Look at this, Ku-yong." I show him my right hand.

He gazes sadly down at my pale hand, covered in my ripped black lace glove like a discarded fish in a dead fisher-man's net.

"Sometimes it's hard for me to hold someone's hand, even when they're right in front of me. I'm still—people are still hard for me."

Before he can take it, I withdraw my hand. I am treating this man who has feelings for me with the bare minimum of politeness. But he doesn't realize that he's the first person I've ever told any of this.

Ku-yong gazes quietly at the space vacated by my hand. He takes something out of his pocket. It's a smudged fountain pen and a yellowed postcard. He begins to draw as if he's alone, his pen scratching like a broom. I haven't seen him like this in a long time, hunched forward, head down, concentrating. I stare at him, mouth agape, content to watch. He's looking at his old pen with affection, like he's Jesus looking at a child.

When he's done he hands me the postcard with a smile. Fine slashes fill the paper, pouring down like shooting stars in the night sky. I laugh despite myself. He's drawn a propaganda leaflet. And it's me he's drawn in it. I look funny and pitiful and cute, all at the same time. I'm wearing a dotted scarf on my head and shaking my fist, chanting slogans, and behind me is the sentence, "Alice! Build up your battle experience to rescue your compatriots!" The propaganda posters and leaflets we were forced to make during the war were fierce, coarse, and foolish. This is different. This is special. I'm intrigued, though I am hardly the type to get provoked by these things. It contains irony and pathos. This is a superlative drawing.

"Are you still—do you still care for him?" Ku-yong lobs the question he's been wondering about. He remembers how restless and resentful I was that summer, pining by the window.

"Not him. Them," I cruelly correct Ku-yong.

It's a low blow to mention men I can barely remember anymore to a man who desperately wants to comfort me. The cheap, artificially carbonated liquor served by the surly barmaid burns, turning my mind blank and clear. Ku-yong's eyes are as dark as ink as he forlornly twists the cap of his fountain pen. I feel torn and a little sorry.

Adequately tipsy like the youth we are, we head back into the night. The dark night of this city, which doesn't yet have electricity fully restored, makes the streetcar stop seem even more desolate. Ku-yong insists he will see me home. He's gallant for a man who's been refused. Maybe he's reliving the sorrow of being turned down.

"When will you get back?" he asks with concern, as though I'm going somewhere far away, although I'm just accompanying Marilyn Monroe to perform for the troops.

"It's a four-day trip, so I should be back at the end of next week."

Ku-yong seems so distressed that I find myself wondering if I will indeed return safely in one piece.

The streetcar barrels towards us, its headlights slicing through the darkness.

Ku-yong puts a hand on my arm. "I'd like to see you when you're back, Ae-sun." His gaze arrests me for a moment.

"Would you like me to say something to Marilyn for you?" I smile, but he doesn't. The streetcar is nearing the stop but his hand is growing heavier on my arm.

He finally lets go and flashes a smile when I try to get on the streetcar. "Please convey my congratulations. And tell her that we are hoping for her happiness, for her to always be happy."

The streetcar takes off and he waves. His wet eyes sparkle as they are swallowed by the black street.

I quickly find a seat so I don't have to see him. But his form follows me, pasted to the window. I turn back and he's still standing there, watching me, growing smaller. What a night. A strange night filled with memories creeping and advancing like fog. I'm not afraid of the regret and disdain settling wetly on my cheeks. I leave behind the man who is perhaps the last person to understand me. I desperately hope he won't remember tonight as remarkable, as a night to be remembered. I hope we can all fall asleep peacefully—all of us, the beggar girl carrying her sibling on her back, the maid seeking abortion funds, lovelorn Yu-ja standing sentry at the dance hall, lonely Mrs. Chang who has to show her husband pictures of naked American women. Seoul adroitly hides its ruins in the darkness and I too disappear into it. I enter the deep blackness of the city, which has chewed and swallowed all of humanity's beauty—the past, the tears, the blood, the lovers, the diaries, the ribbons, the book pages—in equal measure.

Colonial-Style Romance
at the Bando Hotel

July 1947

I GOT OFF THE STREETCAR AND WALKED SELF-consciously in the brown lambskin shoes I had received from my uncle for my twentieth birthday. My gait reflected who I was—light, carefree, and coquettish. Only the heel of my right shoe was worn, and from that you could deduce that I was stubborn and didn't have a great sense of balance. My pale, goosebump-covered calves were revealed all too easily each time the hem of my skirt fluttered. Even if you didn't have an acute sixth sense you would guess that I was on my way to see my lover. That was how carelessly I displayed my passion. I was firmly deluded in believing that the entire world was envious of my romance. I was still a young girl trying my best to look sophisticated. What I didn't realize was that the world had no morals and wasn't interested in one individual. And so, with a truly innocent smile on my face, I walked the streets of Seoul that were brimming with memories of colonization. To my eyes, the streets lined with ginkgo trees—an emblem of Tokyo planted here by the Japanese—were just a splendid sight.

I was in Tokyo when Korea was liberated from Japan. On September 2, 1945, as Japan was signing the Instrument of Surrender on the USS *Missouri* in Tokyo Bay, I was staring at a parcel that had just arrived. I had been planning to go look at the *Missouri*, which was supposed to be unfathomably vast, but the parcel distracted me. A few years later, I had a chance to see the *Missouri* as we were escaping Hungnam; the loud booms of the ship's sixteen-inch artillery made me wet myself several times. Anyway, one of my father's black frockcoats was inside that parcel. It looked like a large dead black bird. Upon receiving the news of my father's death, I'd written home, asking for an item from his closet. Father, a sad, elegant man much like a black bird, left eight frockcoats behind. I stood in front of the mirror to try the coat on. Only then did his death sink in.

The last time I'd seen him was at a teahouse across from Hwasin department store right before I left to study in Japan. He told me not to skip meals and to be sure to get enough sleep. He gave me some money. I said goodbye and left quickly. I'd spotted the dry patches under his eyes and knew he was sickly, but I pretended not to notice. I was embarrassed that people might think I was a mistress receiving money from an old, ill lecher. I suppose it was true that I was his secret paramour—I had stopped being his daughter the moment my mother went back to her family home with me in tow. And I stopped being her daughter when she left me with my grandparents to remarry, joining the family that ran the Sariwon distillery. After that, my grandmother sent me to live with my uncle in Seoul, in Ahyon-dong. My mother had stormed out to escape her situation—the third concubine of the eldest son of a family once listed as one of the richest in Kaesong but now facing ruin—and stopped coming to see me.

Whenever Father happened to be in Seoul, however, he came for a visit. I liked his Leica camera and his collection of French kaleidoscopes, which included erotic blonde dancers performing acrobatics in black undergarments. The world I spied through that small hole was both breathtakingly filthy and beautiful. Hailing from a renowned family of interpreters, he pronounced French words however he wanted to but made them sound authentic. I'd inherited from him certain traits, such as a facility with languages, the disposition of a gambler who would bet a ninety-nine-room house on a single hand, and instincts that valued aesthetics over logic and reason. From my mother I'd inherited my tendency to daydream and my insomnia.

I took off the frockcoat and put it in my suitcase. I decided to leave Tokyo, where I had nobody, and return to Seoul, where nobody was waiting for me. Seoul welcomed me knowingly, both of us filled with hope and fear. I was only qualified to work as a private tutor or waitress but neither fit my aptitudes. My uncle told me that everything remained the same, except the flag flying in front of the former Japanese Government General of Korea building had changed from the Japanese flag to the American one. My uncle had been a pro-Japanese bureaucrat, but he seemed to be doing fine for himself. He showed me a souvenir: a US military flyer that had been dropped from a B-29 right after Korea's liberation. "To the People of Korea," it began, written in Japanese, explaining that the benevolent American military would occupy our country to ensure our happiness, and signed by a Commander Hodge. My uncle made strenuous efforts to cultivate ties with the US military government. He had at one point operated a movie theater in Suwon, so he was able to get me a job at the central film distribution office in the military government, the exclusive distributor of popular Hollywood movies. There, I discovered my talent. I discreetly consulted the dictionary to summarize the plots and translate titles. I handled a range of miscellaneous tasks, the most interesting of which was designing posters and leaflets. My art degree came in handy. I dreamed up the plots for movies I hadn't seen and painted dramatic scenes in the American West with dashing men and beauties. The streets were plastered with posters, printed materials, speeches, and slogans by various political organizations, from the Korea Democratic Party to the provisional government of the Republic of Korea to the Communist Party of Korea to the People's Party of Korea, but in my mind I was lounging on a Santa Monica beach, sipping cocktails. My political involvement was limited to supporting Yo Unhyong solely because of his resemblance to leading men in black-and-white Hollywood films; when he was assassinated I was crushed that we wouldn't see such a good, handsome politician in all of Korea any time soon. In 1946, I got a job through my uncle's connections and went to work at the newly established US public information office. At the time the American military government distributed free printed materials like *Farmers Weekly* and *World News* in order to enlighten the highly illiterate Korean populace. They also created a variety of posters and slogans in order to more effectively reach the illiterate. My hands, which had cut out and pasted Gene Kelly's face on a daily basis, now began drawing public-safety posters about parasite prevention or road safety at the direction of the concerned American regime. I gradually became more rooted in reality.

If I may boast about myself, I would say that my work had made me fairly popular at the time—not as well known as a famous woman poet might have been, but enough that I wasn't discouraged. I was one of the few women who was paid by the US military without having to sell her body. Though I wasn't one of those vain creatures frequenting dance parties at the Bando Hotel, I could see how my circumstances might invite misunderstanding. But I wanted to be the subject of more extensive, complicated misunderstandings and envy. Actually I wanted to be a haughty, picky, and independent modern woman. Or maybe I wanted to be a delicate and innocent girl? Or beautiful and tragic? Or perhaps I wanted to have a baby right away and suckle it, but then I also wanted to make grown men cry and have them grovel at my feet. Maybe instead I wanted to suffer from consumption, coughing bloodily into a white handkerchief. I see now that I had no idea what I wanted, or what kind of person I wanted to be. I was confused and lonely; I just wanted to love someone and felt I would go insane if I wasn't loved in return. I was ready to vanish from the real world in order to immerse myself in love. That was when he appeared before me.

I gulp, thinking about him, but not because of desire. He is no longer alive. My mouth becomes parched. He churns through my brain and leaves ruins behind. He gazes gently into my eyes before ripping through my cornea and spitting on my tears, howling at me. Keeping him with me like this might be making me insane. I quietly waste away as I pretend to lead a quiet life, as though this is the only rational choice I have. It feels like punishment not to be able to look back fondly to happier times, but I keep myself stretched out on a rack.

I met the man I dearly loved and deeply betrayed—Yo Min-hwan—in the summer of '47. If we had crossed paths in our dreams we would have fallen deeply in love and never woken up.

At the cusp of summer, I stopped by the import–export company operating out of the Bando Hotel to help translate English documents at the request of my uncle's friend.

The hotel exuded exotic, colonial sophistication and hypocrisy, and served American officers, foreign business-men, parasitic Korean politicians, and a smattering of mysterious Korean beauties. I entered the hotel and rushed to catch the elevator. The hotel was famous for its pretty elevator operators, but this one was empty.

A man stepped into the elevator after me and stood in the back. "Seven, please." His voice was pleasantly smooth.

I didn't move, feeling his gaze on the back of my neck. I sensed a gentle, cinnamon-scented breeze. That was when the elevator operator rushed in, apologizing. We went up, along with that mysteriously delicate scent. I didn't want to get off on the fourth floor, my stop, when the doors opened. I wanted to turn and look behind me, but I was too nervous and embarrassed.

Not long after that, I was in a crowded elevator at the American military government building when I experi-enced something similar. I felt someone watching me and smelled cinnamon. I didn't get off on my floor. The other passengers got off, one by one, until finally only one person was left behind me. We stood in that elevator, momentarily suspended above ground, listening to each other breathe. What would have happened if I hadn't looked back just then? Would my life have taken a differ-ent turn? But even if I'd known I would turn into stone I would have obeyed my instincts to look. And so I did. He was standing there expectantly as if he had been waiting for a long time for me to turn around. We recognized each other—listening with every fiber of our beings, our hearts thumping, gazing into each other's eyes—and for a moment the rest of the world fell away. The sweet cinnamon scent filled the space as we hovered over reality.

He was the talk of the town. He had studied at Stanford University after graduating from Tokyo Imperial University, and had become a well-regarded translator and author and was an important member of the Korea Writers League. Now he was working in the public information office of the American military government.

"I met Yo Min-hwan," I said dreamily to no one in particular back at the office.

"Who knows what he's really thinking. All he does is smile," someone walking by said, letting slip a hint that I ignored.

Min-hwan, with his rumpled suit and his habit of casually pushing his hair off his forehead, looked gentle at first glance. But his long, rough, limestone-colored face didn't betray any emotions. His eyes were hard to read, his straight nose resembled the handle of a ceramic pot, and his lips were much too smooth. His handsomeness was a mask. He was the prototypical traitor, steeped in certain values while agonizing over others—a Communist working for the American military government. Even when I first met him I sensed he wouldn't be interested in a great, passionate love affair. I could tell he would look down on a naïve, pathetic girl like me, parched for romance. But I was convinced he would end up loving me, not because I was so beautiful or so innocent or so charming, but because I would devote myself utterly to him if given the opportunity. Men instinctively gravitate towards fools like that. The next time I spotted him, I found myself in the grip of a rare flush of confidence and, with nervous sweat beading on my forehead, I approached him to introduce myself, insisting we have tea.

"Why don't we go to the Bando?" he suggested. "I won't make the same mistake again. I should have spoken to you the last time we were in the elevator." He strode forward without looking at me. Perhaps he was embarrassed.

We made awkward, dull conversation, keeping our surging desire at bay. I could feel the waves of passion hurtling towards us. One week later, I got out of his bed, drenched in sweat and tears, and realized I was afloat—a buoy in the middle of the ocean. My heart shrank. Somewhere in that ocean, something dangerous was lurking at the point where our dreams and our despair overlapped. While I had been dreaming of the day I would meet my one great love, he had been hoping the disillusionment he was feeling would pass. And that was precisely the moment I had fallen like an apple by his feet.

That was how our romance began. The secretive nature of our union quickly drew us close. I groomed my eyebrows very thin in an effort to appear more mature, and he kept cutting his chin like a boy who had just learned to shave. Although he was fifteen years my senior, I teased him like he was my younger brother, and each time, he regarded me seriously, like a boy whose feelings had been hurt. I liked him for that. When I teased him he sometimes tugged my earlobes gently.

"I'll tell you your fortune," he would say. "Give me your cup. Hm. I see you'll meet a handsome man." He always read my fortune as we lay in bed drinking cooled coffee, making up what he saw in the coffee grounds at the bottom of my cup. I was always fated to fall in love with him according to the grounds. We did everything in bed—eat, drink, read. It was our entire world.

"I like your moles," I said. "They're like constellations. They should be named after me, since I discovered them."

Tiny moles were scattered on the right side of his face; so small that only a lover lying next to him would be able to see them. I liked touching and gently blowing on them. Those small, brown moles glowed like stars and disappeared magically around dawn. I laughed too much and startled for no reason. He lived alone on the second floor of a Western-style house in Chong-dong, which became filled with my fresh scent and laughter. Our affair continued for over a year. I would wait for him in his room, napping, rifling through his drawers, washing my face. He would return home tired and gaze at me numbly, looking slightly dismayed, as I chattered away. I was a silly child; I never once doubted his love for me. It was all picture perfect.

One day, I watched him from the bed as he changed out of the clothes he'd worn on a business trip and I realized something was amiss. There was one clock in that sunny room of infidelity, and it had stopped at four-thirty, the most ambiguous time of all, the time when you give up on the day.

"My wife is pregnant," he said quietly, his back to me.

I touched my quivering lips. As soon as a mistress loses her sense of self, she loses her dignity. I stood up nonchalantly and went to the window. I wanted to seem worldly. At the time I didn't know that mistresses are as easygoing as prostitutes are virgins. I should have been honest with my feelings and shown him how jealous and resentful and despairing I was. He had been in an unhappy, decade-long marriage. They had had no children, until now. Now, after he had met me. I should have heeded that warning: love could be conceived in a loveless place. I detected something else that hadn't existed in that room until then—guilt. He glanced at me apologetically. I still had a choice at that moment. He was more sympathetic than loving, and I knew that when a man gazes upon a woman with sympathy it means that she has lost him. I should have turned away the moment I detected sympathy in his eyes. But instead I threw myself into his arms, weeping, hanging onto his neck, crying as wretchedly as I could.

"Please stay. I don't expect anything from you. Just stay with me." I held on, casting embarrassment aside. Though in truth I did feel plenty of shame.

He smoothed my wet hair pityingly. I pretended to weep, observing his reactions. A man shouldn't be cocky when a woman hangs on to him tearfully, as she will remember that moment of humiliation forever; it will enable her to betray him. When he embraces an unhappy woman, he would do well to realize that he will always be remembered as part of her unhappiness.

I wanted him out of loneliness and desperation, not pure love. I hoped foolishly that I could hold onto him until he eventually became mine. That this would be recompense for the sorrow I felt that day. In hindsight, I was just a silly young mistress. I didn't hatch my plot out of malice or to put everyone in jeopardy. I don't know why I did what I did next. Why did I betray him? Why did I do the unforgivable?

Welcome to Seoul,
Marilyn Monroe!

February 16, 1954

"STILL, IT WAS REALLY AMAZING. WE HAD TO WAIT TWO weeks for the landmines to be cleared in Wonsan Harbor, and once we landed, Bob Hope and the beautiful ladies welcomed us with open arms!" The driver chatters on excitedly.

"My buddy from high school got a Bronze Star Medal. He said the only reason he survived was because of his helmet," the military policeman sitting next to me chimes in.

"Let me guess—that's where he kept Marilyn Monroe's picture?"

"Bingo! He survived the battle of Changjin, but as soon as he got home he died in a car accident."

"What? That idiot should have gone everywhere with that helmet on."

It's unbearable. The driver keeps taking both hands off the wheel in excitement. We're on our way to meet

Marilyn and nobody is in his right mind. The caravan of cars heading to Yoido Airport begins to speed up competitively. A military truck carrying American soldiers with mass erections kicks up dust to overtake our jeep. Our vehicle charges towards the truck as if it's stealing Marilyn from us. I can't help but get a little excited myself. Things aren't looking good.

As I feared, the usually deserted airport is roiling with humanity. National and international press, American soldiers who have lost their minds, even houseboys—how did they manage to get here? My body reacts instantly upon spotting the single-minded crowd. I grow sweaty and I can't breathe and my hands and feet are stiff. One soldier is so touched that I am a woman, just like Marilyn, that he tries to give me a big embrace. I falter and push through the crowd, looking for Hammett. As the person tasked with all the preparations, Hammett hasn't lost his mind yet.

"You're late!" Hammett says. "Did you talk to the band? Did you check with Taegu Hospital? It's so cold—I hope it's warmer in Taegu. What's wrong? Are you okay?"

My hands are covering my ears. "I really don't feel well. I don't think I can go."

"Now, now. She's landing at any minute! She's probably flying above Suwon right now." Hammett isn't listening to me.

If I foam at the mouth and collapse right this moment, all these men would gratefully step on me to get a better glimpse of Marilyn. My hands still covering my ears, I turn towards the American embassy staff but Hammett grabs me, an expression of slight concern on his face. "Did someone come see you before you left the base?" he whispers.

"Who?"

"Well, the head office was asking about you. About an English-speaking woman who came south from Hungnam on the *Ocean Odyssey*."

Now I am twice as sweaty and nearly panting.

Hammett flashes me a reassuring smile. "It's not a big deal. I'm sure they'll call again if it's something important."

Why are they asking about me? What about the *Ocean Odyssey*? Just thinking about that time is exhausting; my memories of the war are landmines. I'm already nauseated from the racket. The world spins. I turn towards the jeep to sit and take a breath, but suddenly a roar shakes Yoido.

Everyone is craning up. When the four-engine fighter carrying Marilyn appears in the air people are practically rioting. As the aircraft lands, assaulting our eardrums with a boom and causing dust to swirl, I stare down at my feet with my hands over my ears, worried I will be trampled. Hammett grabs me as I'm about to faint and drags me to the front of the crowd. A soldier hits my head with his camera for blocking his view and I respond, "Fuck you." I'm barely standing on my feet. It's so loud I can't hear myself breathing. The ramp is rolled up to the plane. Yoido erupts with cheers and applause. The plane door opens and my eardrums are about to burst.

I see her.

I smile.

I, who didn't really care about seeing her in the first place, find myself shyly smiling at her.

She smiles wider, brighter, more beautiful, like a star.

She stands on the ramp and waves, sweetly responding to the hundreds of American soldiers going crazy. She doesn't forget to kindly greet the cameras pouring light on her. I come to my senses. Marilyn herself is modifying the image I had of her.

She looks even more sensual wearing a flight jacket and fatigues and military boots than she does in a dress. Her military shirt can't hide her voluptuous bosom. She's so dazzling it hurts my eyes. She puts her weight on one foot and pushes her curves out towards the crowd. She puts her hand to her lips and the officer standing behind me groans, calling on God. I take in her blonde hair, thick, bright, moving with the breeze. Her face appears more natural than it does in the movies, but the color of her hair doesn't. What would she look like if her hair were a different color, without that overdone icing? In movies, important events and conflicts begin with blondes. Brunettes can seduce and ruin men, too, but blondes can do that without even trying. I'm feeling a little jealous. I feel a little betrayed as the lovelorn GIs, whom I normally consider to be equivalent to insects, call her name. But I follow suit and call out, too. Welcome, Miss Monroe! Welcome to Korea, which has turned into a mass grave from three years of bloody battle!

I watch as Marilyn finishes shaking hands with the military brass and speaks with reporters. The publicist who accompanied her from Japan finds me. "Please get these trunks to the helicopter. Don't lose them!"

I am about to get the MPs to move them to the helicopter, but I realize I'm holding two feminine brick-colored leather trunks. "Didn't Miss Monroe's husband come, too? Mr. Joe DiMaggio?"

"No, she came alone."

"Aren't they on their honeymoon?"

"Yes, but Mr. DiMaggio decided to stay in Tokyo."

I'm suddenly curious about this Joe DiMaggio. Some nerve to send his wife to these soldiers during their honeymoon. Especially when his wife is Marilyn Monroe. I have a lot of respect for this famous professional baseball player, although I think he's made a fatal mistake. I guarantee he'll regret this day for the rest of his life.

"Whew. I like your gloves!" Marilyn deigns to notice as she grabs my black-lace-gloved hand to hop into the helicopter. My glove looks so filthy and her hand is so cold.

The men—the USO staff, the photographers, the officers—are fussing over seat assignments and lose the opportunity to display their chivalry to Marilyn.

Hammett introduces me to Marilyn, who flashes a golden smile. "A lovely name, Alice. Nice to meet you." Her husky voice melts in my ears. It's overly sweet, like in the movies, and fragile, like a cookie dunked for too long in a cup of tea.

I stare in a daze as Marilyn shakes hands with the men crowding the doorway. It's as if I'm in a movie myself. I feel self-conscious, but then the fact that I will never be more than a supporting character around Marilyn brings me back to earth.

Marilyn sneezes and the men fuss, looking incredibly sad and concerned. I push through them and settle her in her seat.

"Are you all right? Aren't you cold?" I hand her a blanket.

She shivers and holds it close. "It's colder here than in Tokyo."

"Yes, spring comes sooner to Tokyo. Would you like coffee? You have to finish it before we take off, though." I hand her the coffee I've brought.

She's pleased, wrapping her hands around the tin cup. "Have you been to Tokyo?"

"Yes, I studied there. Before the war. I mean—before liberation. I mean—anyway, it was a long time ago."

"Oh! Joe is in Tokyo right now. My husband," she explains, showing me her wedding ring.

"It's beautiful." Making a fuss in these situations is expected in the world of women but I can't start doing something I've never done just because I'm with Marilyn Monroe. I praise the craftsmanship of the ring, but she doesn't seem to expect a girlish, fake gesture. "It would have been nice if he came with you," I say, not really meaning it. If he did all those soldiers would be beaten to death by baseball bat.

"He's so tired. The flight to Tokyo was so long! He actually wanted a small wedding. He's probably resting at the hotel right now. It's a wonderful place. It's in ... Gin—what's the name—"

"Oh, Ginza? The Imperial Hotel? He won't be bored there."

Marilyn looks anxious somehow, and the word "wedding" seems to stick awkwardly to her mouth. It's as alien as pronouncing "ammonite" or "Rio de Janeiro" is for me.

"We're going to Taegu, an important southern city. The best actresses of Korea will be waiting to welcome you at the airport."

Marilyn is surprised. "Actresses?"

"Yes, Choi Eun-hee and Paek Song-hee."

Marilyn falls silent at the unpronounceable Korean names.

"They're wonderful actresses, just like you." I flinch as I finish that sentence. I don't recall Marilyn's actual acting skills—I only remember her breathy voice and her curves—but I give a bald lie.

Marilyn gives me a faint, routine smile at this insulting comparison to Korean actresses.

To hide my embarrassment I offer her another cup of coffee, but she turns it down. A hefty nurse officer with a mustache named Betty rushes in and shouts that we need to leave. She orders the photographers off and yells at me to sit down, citing the safety rules of the aircraft. The helicopter finally lifts off, pitching and rolling, and

Marilyn asks, "By the way, Alice, your English is so good. Where did you learn it?"

I know my answer will be buried by the noise of the propeller, but I still raise my voice to shout, "From Joseph! His name was Joseph!"

The name of the second man I loved. The propeller shreds that name and scatters it into the blue sky.

"Look, they're like peas boiling in a pot!" Marilyn laughs as Betty points out the welcoming masses gathered at Taegu's Tongchon Airport.

The khaki balaclavas on the soldiers' heads do make them resemble peas. Marilyn sniffled during our flight but seems more sprightly now.

The roar from Tongchon Airport is similar to that of Yoido Airport. I place a hand on my chest and breathe, trying to keep calm. I desperately wish that the black terror that overcomes me every time I gaze upon a mass of humanity would bypass me today. I pray I can avoid the shame of fainting flat on my back in front of Marilyn Monroe and all these people.

I'm still trying to tame my nerves when Marilyn opens the door and enters the crowd. Her name roars up to the sky. Camera flashes tumble forward like an avalanche as Marilyn smiles confidently, smothered by sharp white shards of light. She leans forward to wave at someone far back in the crowd and sighs erupt from all over. Koreans in the crowd are jumping up and down, also excited to see Choi Eun-hee and Paek Song-hee. It's chaos. I fight my way through and introduce the actresses to Marilyn. Marilyn greets them in a friendly way and links arms with them. She seems so alien next to the hanbok-clad actresses, but her warm, friendly demeanor instantly wins everyone over. Though she doesn't know much about Korea, she understands people; she doesn't need to speak the language. Her attractive physicality renders my fumbling interpretation unnecessary.

While Marilyn gives interviews I rush to the camp with a USO staff member. We careen down the new road, kicking up dust, weaving around Quonset huts lined up below a pine forest. Soldiers gather for the performance with cameras hanging around their necks, as innocent and excited as if they are going home to see their mothers.

Who knows who wrote the sign hanging on the hospital entrance, WELCOME MARILYN, but you can tell how excited they were, judging by the energy in the letters. Patients who would normally be lying in bed are pomading their hair eagerly, the wards enflamed with joyous excitement.

"If you tell them Marilyn isn't coming they'll start rioting," a Korean nurse officer says, shaking her head.

The other Korean nurses giggle and ask me if I've seen Marilyn Monroe and whether she is as pretty as she is in pictures.

"Did you choose a soldier to talk to her and take a picture?" I ask.

"Does it really have to be the most handsome one?" asks the nurse officer disapprovingly.

The nurses giggle again and let me peek around the curtain to see the soldier they have selected. He's not just handsome; he's the spitting image of Clark Gable.

"What's the point of being handsome?" grouses the nurse officer. "Look what happened to him. It happened while he was shoveling shit."

The Clark Gable lookalike was using gasoline to clean frozen pipes in the bathroom when he caused an explosion, giving him burns on the lower half of his body. Although he looks like a movie star, he can't talk about that experience in front of a reporter.

"What about the soldier who cries every day? His twin brother died at Pork Chop Hill and his mother is very ill back home."

The young soldier from Oregon isn't as handsome as Clark Gable but he has a sob story that would inspire patriotism. He's selected as the lucky fellow who will receive a kiss and a gift from Marilyn.

She arrives as I examine the makeshift stage improvised by the shabby hospital. I can tell from the roar. I peer out of the window to see the jeep carrying Marilyn barreling towards the hospital. Soldiers chase after it, waving. I wonder if they ran that excitedly when Commander MacArthur himself came for a visit. Marilyn is standing in the jeep, waving back, and the gloomy barracks now look like a movie set.

A bright halo surrounds her as she walks into the dark hospital; a patient on the brink of death might think an angel has come to take him. Of course, that's because of the flashes from the cameras that follow her around. She banishes the ominous smell of rubbing alcohol that floats around the hospital with her bright blonde hair, her pale forehead, and her red lips. The hospital soon descends into mayhem, crowded as it is with patients, army surgeons, nurses, and workers from the base. Marilyn makes her rounds from bed to bed, hugging the patients and wishing for their quick recovery. "God bless you," she says in a kind, serious voice.

A weepy Italian American soldier from the 1st Navy Division clings to Marilyn, rubbing his lips against her cheek, and her touch is gentle, not even betraying what I assume would be displeasure. He was supposed to be transferred to a hospital in Tokyo yesterday but he had waited to meet her. The most sensual saint in the history of humanity smooths the soldier's white sheet. The war is over but the soldiers are still here, country boys who came all the way here from America, not knowing what war really is. Marilyn speaks with the soldier who lost his twin and suffered a leg injury in a battle near the 38th Parallel. The cameras flash in a frenzy as Marilyn holds his hand. As they exchange pleasantries, the soldier looks around furtively and whispers something in her ear. His eyes dart before he fixes his gaze on the ceiling. Marilyn seems a little surprised, then kisses him on the cheek. "Don't worry. I'm sure you'll be back home soon." She gives him the chocolates she brought as a present and the soldier says goodbye, looking pale.

We decide we need to start the show immediately when we see that the soldiers with casts on their legs are struggling and grunting like Frankenstein's monster to gather around her. We quickly head to the plywood stage near the barracks. After a quick chat with the band that has already warmed up, Marilyn acknowledges the applause and sings George Gershwin and Buddy De Sylva's "Do It Again."

"Oh, do it again … waiting for you …" Her voice is sickly sweet and damp and overtly seductive. It makes your knees buckle. I look at her in surprise. Her first show in Korea is incredibly shabby but she herself isn't. I was doubtful she could do anything worthwhile on that piece of plywood without any spotlights but she's proving me wrong. She's a well-trained actress, and though her voice isn't that powerful, she's embodying her appeal with every gesture. You can't do that if you're not smart. Does she hide her sensibilities behind the face of a dumb blonde? Her breathy tone is certainly exaggerated but she's not your average actress. Her brilliance is unconstrained as she kisses and signs the cast of a soldier who is agog in her presence.

As soon as this small but moving performance is over, we move on by helicopter. Marilyn seems to have just noticed that she was singing in the cold on the opposite side of the earth. Her face is flushed. "Alice, aren't we going to see any cities or towns in Korea?"

I can't bear to tell her that the cities and towns have pretty much all burned down. "No, that's what these shows are. You go from base to base. You must be tired. How is your cold? You should take something for it."

"No, I'm all right. I smelled a lot of medicine at the hospital so I'm feeling fine," she jokes, smiling.

I tell her about the Clark Gable lookalike. "When the toilet exploded it shot into the air. Like Dorothy's house in *Wizard of Oz*. It spun in the sky."

Marilyn laughs. "Oh my! Why didn't I meet him? You know, Clark Gable is my idol. He's my favorite!"

"Well, if the toilet is gone with the wind, how would Clark Gable feel?"

Marilyn laughs politely at my lame joke.

I ask her what the soldier whispered in her ear.

"Actually he said something odd. He said his dead brother keeps appearing in his dreams. And other dead comrades. I don't know what he was talking about. He was a signal corpsman, I think." She squints. "He told me that his dead superior's voice once cut in during a communication, and he saw himself dead. For a while an Oriental man wearing a black hat was following him around. Could that be real?"

"I'm not sure. In the West, death holds a scythe, right? I wonder if he was talking about our death, who wears a black hat."

"I wished him luck, and he did for me, too."

I have nothing to say to that. For a soldier going mad, trying to avoid death, luck is valuable, but I don't know that Marilyn needs it.

* * *

We get off the helicopter and get on a truck to head to the 45th Division, and we are stunned by the parade of military trucks zooming up from below the slope, kicking up dust.

An MP hurries us along, laughing. "Everyone in the surrounding villages is terrified, thinking war has broken out again. Ten thousand American navy men are on their way here, so the civilians are packing to flee!"

I can't breathe. I can already smell their sweat, which reeks of Lucky Strikes and the ground beef that comes in one-gallon cans. The reason for this disturbance has her arms around the drivers' shoulders, taking countless pictures with them. The overcast sky settles lower and lower and the wind is shifting gloomily. It looks like rain or maybe even snow.

In contrast to the first stage, on which the band members were afraid to step backward in case they fell off, this large stage is outdoors. Singers and dancers have gotten ready for the show in the makeshift dressing room hastily created with black velour curtains. On the stage an MC who looks like Fred Astaire is cracking jokes as the soldiers hoot and applaud. The audience's voices billow louder. Their hollering dampens the band's music.

As the makeup artist seats Marilyn at a small vanity, Captain Walker, who is in charge of the shows, enters, looking flustered. "That song wasn't on the set list," he says to me in a low voice. "'Do It Again.'"

"Miss Monroe decides what she sings," I tell him.

Marilyn asks what's going on.

PEMBROKE BRANCH TEL. 6689575

"We need to change the repertoire," Captain Walker says seriously. "It's a little provocative to sing 'Do It Again' in front of the boys, don't you think? How about something more classic?"

I manage to swallow my laughter. Doesn't he know that even "Ave Maria" is seductive when Marilyn sings it?"

"It *is* a classic. It's George Gershwin," Marilyn says calmly.

"We're going to have to change it," the captain insists.

Marilyn's smile falls off her face as she turns away. She would be no different from anyone else if sensuality were erased from her voice. But the captain is being rude. You can't ever be honest when you praise or criticize a woman. Women know whether they are beautiful or whether they are wise. We know this instinctively. I can see from Marilyn's expression that she knows her own decadent, lewd appeal.

"How about this?" she offers. "I'll change it from 'Do It Again' to 'Kiss Me Again.'"

The captain frowns but acquiesces. "Please don't make it too provocative."

"Captain, it's just a kiss."

As they come to a meaningless agreement, an officer rushes in. "We need to get you on stage right now. We can't keep them waiting. They're throwing rocks out there!"

It's true; the tenor of the shouting outside has turned into something more sinister. We have to raise our voices to hear ourselves talk. I take a peek. It's really something.

The MC is flustered. At the sight of the men, Marilyn flushes and looks uncertain. Though she receives five thousand letters a week from soldiers, she must not have imagined what it would be like on the ground.

"Here's your dress," I say, finding her costume from her trunk. I don't want to be pelted by rocks. I take out a blue silk dress that sparkles beautifully like the night ocean reflecting stars. I furtively hold it up to myself as I bring it to her. If I put it on I would look both tragic and farcical. When she puts on the dress, the change is dramatic, with her pale skin, generous bosom, and curves on full display, and I find myself wanting to know more about her.

"Will you be okay? It looks like it will snow." I'm suddenly worried.

The dress, with its plunging neckline, is so thin that it can't hide the blue goosebumps on her translucent skin. She has thick makeup on but feverish heat seeps from her forehead and from under her nose. I worry she might collapse onstage.

"It's fine. The show must go on." She slides her feet into strappy sandals.

At this point, even tanks would be unable to control the soldiers. Finally the MC calls out her name and the place erupts in cheers. The earth shakes.

Snow flutters like white flower petals as Marilyn stands in the middle of the stage. Her blonde hair renders all other women meaningless—the brunettes and the redheads and the raven-haired. She pouts, sticks her chest out, and shimmies. I'm deafened by the roar. I realize I was worried for no reason. She has to stand on stage, no matter how feverish and ill she is; she has to be in front of an audience no matter how lonely, misunderstood, and rejected she might feel. Her fate might be to love all men while not receiving a single man's love. I can't criticize her; after all, I wasn't able to love even one man. The chorus members in red jackets stand next to her as she gets into the groove. How does it feel to be up there? I'm terrified just seeing all these people in uniforms. Not because they're testosterone-filled American soldiers but because they're people. Marilyn is singing "Diamonds Are a Girl's Best Friend" from the movie. I wonder who her best friend is—a man who buys her diamonds? Except the man would leave and the diamonds themselves would probably be fake. A beautiful woman doesn't have any friends, as neither men nor women want to be friends with her. Men want to fall in love and women want to judge, and everyone wants to blame the beautiful woman for being the seductress. She shouldn't be sad that she doesn't have any friends; if she had some, she'd eventually figure out that they're actually her enemies.

The day's excitement has settled a bit but it's still festive in the cafeteria, where Marilyn is serving soldiers. She's thrilled when a round cake with her name written in pink icing is brought out. The Korean cooks who baked it are introduced and she hugs them and takes a picture with them. Marilyn hasn't changed out of her dress yet. I see that she's perspiring. We're all worried she is going to collapse but she keeps telling us she is fine.

"Alice!" she calls. "Come, meet the captain who speaks Japanese! Alice lived in Japan, too. When was it again?"

The captain who was chatting with Marilyn looks at me. "*Konbanwa*," he says. He tells me in Japanese he was a Japanese interpreter during the Second World War. During the early days of the war, when interpreters were scarce, he helped Koreans communicate with the UN troops. He also speaks Spanish and had been stationed with the mostly Puerto Rican 65th Regiment. He raises his glass. "*Salud!*"

"Both of you speak Japanese so well!" exclaims Marilyn.

I don't want to cause dismay when she finds out that Korea was a colony, so I don't tell her that. She asks the captain about Tokyo. Her mind is on Tokyo. Of course, a wife's heart is with her husband, but she looks so happy and free right now. It's easy to forget she's feeling unwell.

Betty interrupts. "Marilyn, that's enough. You have to change at the very least."

Marilyn rubs her hot forehead and agrees. "Have you seen my small makeup bag?"

"It's probably in the dressing room," I tell her.

We help her back to the room so she can change into a sweater and a pair of slacks. She looks at herself in the mirror as she changes, as if disappointed that there is only one. Betty and I are too tired to be impressed by her physique; we pack up while glancing at her voluptuous curves.

"I can't find it," Marilyn says, alarmed.

Betty goes outside to search and I dig around the messy dressing room. "Don't worry," I tell her. "We'll find it."

Marilyn nods, biting her lip. She's wrapped a blanket around herself. She's trembling. "I don't know if I can sleep after such an exciting day."

"It was wonderful. You were beautiful," I say sincerely, though she might be tired of all the praise.

"I've never sung in front of so many people," Marilyn confesses shyly, blushing. "I've never gotten so much applause."

"Really? You must experience this all the time." I'm genuinely surprised.

"No, today was very special," she says dreamily, hugging her knees. "I felt alive. I'm never going to forget it."

"Maybe it's because they're soldiers," I offer. "Soldiers are always more passionate."

She doesn't hear me, perhaps still luxuriating in the cheers.

The passionate applause rings in my ears, too. My heart aches for the soldiers who won't be able to fall asleep tonight, thinking about her beautiful form.

"Do you have jewelry or money in the bag?" I ask.

Marilyn looks distracted, and I see a familiar anxiety flash across her face. "No—I have some medicine in it, that's all."

"Something you need for sleeping?" I ask cautiously, acting on my hunch.

Marilyn nods. I open my handbag, take out a small coin purse, and fish out a few phenobarbital pills. She laughs with delight, then leans close and whispers confidentially, "Alice, do you have trouble sleeping, too?"

I can tell I'm blushing. I think I understand how men must feel when they encounter her breathy voice. I can even understand their wives' jealousy. "Sometimes. I get these from a friend who works at a clinic. She doesn't like that I take them."

"Thank you, Alice. Truly." Marilyn gives me a hug and takes the pills from my hand. These sleeping pills are a better friend than diamonds for those of us who want to forget their past.

Our eyes meet and she smiles. We are instantly closer.

She takes out her earrings and stretches her legs. "The actresses from the airport were so elegant and beautiful. I want to see their movies."

"They are true actresses. You're filled with energy when you watch their plays. It's amazing."

"Do you enjoy plays, too?" Marilyn asks.

"I used to see a lot of them a long time ago. Ibsen and Shakespeare and Chekhov."

"You like Chekhov, too! My acting teacher, Michael Chekhov, is Anton's nephew. I really respect him." Marilyn springs up with delight.

I'm surprised she has an acting teacher. "He must be wonderful," I say.

"I learned so much from him," she says. "Like the limits of my acting."

"Limits?"

"He said I'm so sensual that it's hard for me to show audiences something more than that." She says this lightly, but I feel immensely sad for her because I know it's true.

I can't think of what to say so I just blurt out whatever pops into my head. "I don't know. Just because you're an actor doesn't mean you need to play every part equally well. Isn't it true that an actor is best at one kind of role? Like it is for writers—even if they write a lot, there is just one story they want to tell." Am I really telling her that her fate is to play coquettes for the rest of her life?

Marilyn lowers her eyes. Her lashes look like the wings of a descending bird. "I suppose that makes sense. You sure know a lot about actors and writers."

"I used to be in love with a writer," I confess without realizing it. I'm honest only to someone I will never see again.

"Really! Alice, how exciting! Do tell me about him."

I'm already regretting it. "They say you should never even be friends with a writer because you'll find yourself in their work."

"I always wish directors and writers would really get to know me and write about the real me," she says seriously.

"But that can be dangerous. You'll hate yourself when you see yourself in someone's work. And he will end up hating the character while he is writing. That is a writer's limit, isn't it?" My tone is bitter.

She smiles mysteriously, the kind deployed by someone who doesn't have enough time or experience to under-stand the person they are talking to.

I smile awkwardly. My English isn't the best but it's not that she can't understand me. She might simply be the type who's not convinced by anyone. We are both women who are partial to our own emotions; I can guess that much from my fellow comrade-in-phenobarbital.

Betty walks in. "Alice, your boss is looking for you."

Marilyn nods for me to go. I quickly head outside. I was wondering where Hammett was. I haven't seen him since the afternoon. Earlier I asked him to take me to the orphanage that might have news about Chong-nim, since we're down in Taegu anyway. The card that the chairman's wife gave me in the dance hall burns in my coat pocket. I need to speak to that nun. We must be going there now. My hands are clammy with anticipation. I might find out more about Chong-nim tonight.

I run towards Hammett, who is standing under the security light in front of the building. "Hammett! Where were you today?"

He turns around, his expression wooden under the yellow light. "Alice, remember I mentioned that people wanted to talk to you?" He sounds tense.

"Is it the intelligence bureau? What is it about?" I'm nervous.

Hammett holds my elbow, his grip firm. "Yes, but—before that you need to see someone else. You—it might be a surprise—" he trails off, looking hard into my eyes.

"Who is it?" My voice trembles as I try to smile. I swallow. My heart is dancing with a premonition of sorts. I'm tense and calm at the same time, as if I have been waiting for this moment. I thought there was no longer anything that could possibly shock me, but who is it that wants to see me on this cold, dark, February night? The wind stabs my lungs and digs in deep but I'm okay. I feel hot. I hear footsteps, familiar, firm footsteps, now across from me under the yellow light.

"It's been a long time," the man wearing all gray says to me, the light perched on his head like a hat.

My mouth reacts before my head. "Joseph."

His face is bright under the light.

Joseph.

My English teacher, my second lover, the friend of my first lover, my sanctuary, my Bible, my regret, my riddle. He is standing here.

"Alice," he says again, calling me by the very name he gave me.

The Other Man

August 1948

ON AUGUST 15, 1948, THE AMERICAN MILITARY government regime in Korea came to an end. That was when everything between Min-hwan and me ended, too. Nothing had changed from the outside; I was still a coquettish girl whose whereabouts after work were suspect, and he was still my secret lover. But invisible cracks had begun to form. The collapse of a relationship doesn't begin on the day you part ways; it builds gradually, starting on the day you witness each other's truths.

As a parade was being held in the plaza of the capitol building to commemorate the establishment of the government of the Republic of Korea, I lay entwined in our bed sheets, reading a short story of his that had been published in a literary magazine. It was the first work of fiction he had produced in two years, during which time he had written nothing but political critiques and published translations.

"She is ruled by animalistic instinct … it would be better if she were biased, but her intellect doesn't reach that level … her pathetic, immature nature …"

The story had nothing of the quality of his earlier work. It skipped equally over ideology and artistry, but I detected an element of honesty in it. I was embarrassed and angry; I had to put the magazine down several times. The story centered on a boring male labor activist who led a life on the lam, but I spotted myself in a dancer of a music troupe, whom he is trying to reform. The half page describing the dancer was all about me. The passage didn't include identifying markers, so he could certainly insist that I wasn't his inspiration, but I could tell that this was how he felt about me.

"Just as I cannot leave this place, the same is true with my relationship with her. She will twine herself around me and never let me go …"

The woman in the story was placid but lustful. Yet despite her many flaws, she was the woman the protagonist loved the most. She wasn't respectable but she was adored. That was true in real life, too. Min-hwan was my protector; our relationship emitted a strong whiff of incest. Once, Min-hwan had asked me about my father, and I told him he had been as kind as he was. He wrinkled his nose, looking hurt. I pretended I didn't understand what I was doing, but of course I did. I could be the adult daughter he never had. I was the sole flaw in a man who acted as if he was a paragon of morality. I stayed by his side despite understanding this truth at the heart of our relationship. In a pitiable attempt at revenge against what I perceived to be his self-centeredness, I refused to worry myself with whether he would feel guilty about our love affair.

To be sure, I was just one small part of all of his concerns. Long before the Republic of Korea was established, Min-hwan quit working for the American military government. I never understood why he worked for the Americans in the first place, but that didn't mean I wasn't puzzled when he quit.

"I guess you should have studied Turgenev, not Wordsworth," I teased. "You would have been on the right side, then."

"Learning a language isn't something to joke about," he admonished me seriously. "I chose to learn English as a rebellion against having to learn Japanese when they were in charge, but then I was drawn to it. I don't think it's necessary to speak many languages. It's like believing in more than one God."

"What are you talking about?" I protested. "Knowing English guarantees your future."

"You say that because you don't know what it's like in America. They'll teach you their language but they'll keep everything else for themselves."

I didn't understand how he could feel so conflicted about America. He left his post as matter-of-factly as if he had concluded an experiment in which he was the subject. He quit working for the Americans, unwilling to compromise his beliefs any longer. At that time both the left and the right were stealthily gearing up for battle. With the victory of the right wing, the suppression of the Communist Party became more visible. Min-hwan's fellow writers who belonged to the Workers' Party of South Korea began to head north.

"I'll go with you," I offered. Several of his friends were disappearing north with their mistresses, not fully understanding what their abandoned wives and children would face in the coming years.

Min-hwan snapped at me for the first time. "Stop! This is the best place for you, even if it isn't perfect."

"My mom is up north, I am not religious, and I'm not wealthy anymore. I could have a nice life up there. Why won't you go with me? Is it because of your family?"

Min-hwan sighed and looked at me pityingly for a long time. In the following years I would miss that gaze. I liked that dark, damp gaze so much that I would purposely bring out his sadness. I knew it was cruel. But I liked how solitary and bereft he looked when I mentioned his family, and so I tormented and teased him just to see that gloomy expression. I would take his family photo out of his notebook, put it on the table, and pretend to drop it.

"Remember last year, when the women's director in the military government talked about how patriotic groups were mobilized during Japanese rule to find people with concubines? I heard it's the same now; they won't hire officials with concubines. Your luck has run out," I would tease, comparing myself to a concubine.

He didn't laugh and I didn't either. My teasing didn't contain irony, the most important factor in creating laughter. His situation was so banal that even a cheap weekly magazine wouldn't be interested in it as a story. Here he was, a well-educated man in an arranged marriage, who left his wife and child in his hometown to keep a young mistress in the city. I looked and acted the part of a modern woman but my persistent innermost desires were far from modern. Although I shouldn't have wasted time thinking about the aspects of his life I wasn't privy to, I imagined his wife's pale neck, his daughter's chubby feet, and their tea table glowing with domestic harmony. His wife never came to Seoul and he visited Chonju to see them only once a month.

When he went home, I tagged along to Seoul Station to see him off, even though he hated it when I did.

"Have a good trip," I would say, pretending to weep. "Think about me from time to time."

He would give a dispirited laugh and we would sit apart on a bench as we waited for the train. Day students in school uniforms and old-fashioned aristocrats wearing traditional hats and frightened country girls balancing bundles on their heads, who would eventually become maids or prostitutes, would stream past us. They were rooted in the reality of the train station, while we resided in the romantic realm. When the train pulled into the station, he would give my hand a hard squeeze then go out through the gate without looking back. I would quietly stroke the place he had been sitting, touching the guilt he left behind, feeding the fluttering in my heart.

In an affair, guilt is an aphrodisiac. Were we really that sad and despairing? Did we suffocate each other, savoring those emotions? All I know is that we wanted each other until we grew tired, and we didn't stop even when we did. He was by my side during that time of my life; a foolish time that everyone should experience at least once.

And then someone else entered our relationship.

Joseph, the man who named me Alice.

But I still don't know his real name.

The Fateful Triangle

May 1949

MIN-HWAN DIDN'T GO NORTH. HE PUBLISHED A FEW articles, harshly criticizing the dogma of the US military government, and returned to his alma mater in Tokyo to compile an academic journal of English literature, which he had done when he was a student. Left behind in Seoul, I spent my days feeling anxious, not just because he wasn't there but because I finally saw the state our society was in once I stepped back from our cocooned world. A man I'd studied with in Tokyo suggested I join the Korean Art Association, which had changed its name along with the establishment of the Korean government. Everyone in the South seemed to be joining associations and leagues. I smiled awkwardly at him, and he advised me that I couldn't remain politically and ideologically uninterested in today's world. I asked him a silly question as a joke: did people who love humanity go north and people who love art stay in the South? I wasn't deeply committed to either and so couldn't easily make a decision. He laughed at me, sneering at me not because of my lifestyle but because I wasn't a great artist. It made sense; I myself looked down on him not because of his unsavory character but because he was simply a bad artist.

He wasn't aware that I was secretly filled with strong artistic opinions and positions. I talked as if I wasn't quite sure of my talents, but that was out of modesty, a gesture of self-protection. Once, another artist saw a poster I'd drawn and demanded to know why I didn't make true art. Of course, those posters were primarily functional, so it was hard to spot my artistic viewpoint, but I did create them. I liked my work. I was that rare propaganda artist who was politically naïve. The slogans and symbols I worked hard at creating clearly and thoroughly served this or that ideology, but I didn't subscribe to any of it. I was free. My work was the product of my artistic taste, one that valued a concise, economical line and a balanced composition. As an artist I hoped humanity could better itself. Earnestly I drew posters encouraging illiterate old folks living in the mountains to vote, worrying and experimenting and feeling delight. I waited anxiously for a version of myself that would someday become complete, as though I were an unknown, stuttering actress who hadn't yet landed the perfect part.

When he was away, I discovered in myself someone freer. That made me scared and anxious. While I missed him desperately, a part of me realized that life without him was possible. I blocked that thought as I waited impatiently for him to return. The night before he was due back, I went to his place with fresh-cut flowers to liven up his room. I had my keys in my hand when I noticed the front door was open a crack. I flung open the door and ran in.

Two men were in the room. A leather suitcase lay on its side. Still in his travel clothes and with a brown jacket over his arm, Min-hwan was standing by the window, looking angry. He flinched in surprise when he spotted me. The other man, in a black suit, was seated in a chair, and he stood and turned to look at me, as embarrassed as if he had entered a funeral late. He quickly recovered his composure and smiled. Flustered, I studied this man's face for a few minutes.

He was tall and handsome, with very pale skin as if blood was leaching slowly out of his body. His brown eyes stood out against his pale complexion and black hair. I could sense a prickly, wild nature hiding behind his gentle demeanor. He had straight teeth and his sharp eyes below his dark brows were observant. I walked forward hesitantly before stopping. He seemed neither Oriental nor white, but some new race God created for his own convenience.

Finally Min-hwan broke the silence. "This is Joseph," he said stiffly, gesturing at the man awkwardly.

Joseph said hello in both English and Japanese.

"Do you not speak Korean?" I asked in Korean.

He answered in English. "I'd like to learn. Will you teach me?" His quick, bright smile was disarming and his tone was kind and witty.

"How do you two know each other?" I asked.

The two men glanced at each other, and Min-hwan primly turned his head away. Joseph grinned. "I think of him as a friend, but he must not think the same of me."

Joseph went on to tell me more about himself. Whenever I didn't understand his English, Min-hwan translated tersely. Who knew why he was so displeased, but his grumpiness felt bracing. Joseph Pines was his full name, he said, and explained that he was the happy ending to a *Madame Butterfly*-like romance, born to an American officer who had fallen in love with a Japanese woman. During his happy childhood he frolicked around the foreigners' cemetery in Yokohama. His family left for America when he reached school age. He led the life of an average American boy, graduated from college, got a job, and, one day, felt compelled to return to Japan.

"Did you meet Mr. Yo in Japan?" I asked in Japanese.

"Mr. Yo went to college with a friend of mine, and he introduced us when I was looking for a Korean friend. We got along immediately." Joseph gave Min-hwan a fond glance as Min-hwan waved him off, scowling.

I found myself feeling jealous. "What brings you to Korea?"

Joseph grew more serious, telling me about his role as a businessman and missionary—the first to land in any newly conquered land, I thought, along with disease. His words were warm and his eyes sparkled with intelligence.

"It suits you," I agreed. "You're not planning to be a

minister, are you? You're too young, and the girls won't leave you alone!"

"How did you know? Being a man of faith draws young women to open their hearts to you even when you're old."

We laughed as if we were old friends. I could feel Min-hwan staring at me, surprised at my uncharacteristic vitality. I was thrilled; he was jealous. We continued to banter. Our conversation was a dizzy mix of English, Japanese, and Korean. By the end, as I grew tired from the volley of three languages, the three of us had become fast friends.

Our love triangle was one that sparkled with youth, a triangle that could let out a clear sound thanks to a small gap in the structure. Soon, though, that gap would be filled with misunderstanding, lust, and envy, the clear ringing sound turning sharp and plosive as they tormented us. Even now, I can feel the shock of Min-hwan's cold, burning gaze as he took in my nude body, tangled in the sweat-soaked bed with Joseph, on the day he walked in on us. Of course, I should have run after him and hung onto him, conveying my futile remorse through tears. But I couldn't. Joseph and I were joined together, in the position of betrayal. I don't know how we ended up that way—no, that's not true, I think we knew we would from the first day we met. All three of us had been very skilled actors as we laughed in three languages.

There hadn't been a friendship. Not even for a moment.

* * *

In the weeks following Min-hwan's return from Tokyo, Joseph was busy. He traveled around the country for his missionary work and also went to Japan from time to time to take care of his business there. When in Seoul he stayed with a middle-aged American missionary in Ahyon-dong, where there was a sizeable population of missionaries. She lived in a Japanese-built house, close to where I was staying at my uncle's. I was the first person Joseph came to see when he was in town, and my family was kind to him, treating him with fondness and approving of his gentlemanly ways.

"Teach me Korean and I'll teach you English," Joseph suggested one day, and I accepted his request to officially become his Korean instructor. We would no longer use Japanese when we were together. I hoped I could land a better job opportunity if I brushed up on my English. Maybe I would even be able to go to America to continue my studies. Joseph introduced me to his friend Hammett, who worked at the American public information office, and asked him to look after me like his own sister. Hammett looked me up and down begrudgingly, but years later he kept his word. When I went to him after the war, bedraggled and unhinged, Hammett clucked sympathetically as he welcomed me with open arms.

Our lessons were interesting and free-flowing. I gave him a funny, Koreanized version of his name, Chu Cho-sop.

"Ae-sun ... For you ... I know! What about Alice? It sounds similar to Ae-sun and it suits you well."

Those became our code names. We called each other by our new names when we were together. Joseph would sit in that low-ceilinged tatami room furnished with a low bed and table, earnestly reading children's textbooks out loud. The room would fill with his hesitant voice and my awkward breathing. Joseph was still unfailingly kind and polite but now that I was getting to know him better I suspected that his geniality was a disguise masking coldness. I didn't mind. A man who suppressed his nature was both dangerous and attractive. We would banter and joke, but when our eyes met he would quickly turn away. I began to have questions about him. Why was he learning Korean from me, anyway? He could have asked anyone else. He grew quieter and quieter as we spent more and more time together. It didn't take long for me to take that silence as an invitation.

"You two are wasting your time," Min-hwan said, displeased that I was growing closer to Joseph.

"Isn't he your friend? Why do you have a problem with him?"

Min-hwan frowned each time I uttered the word "friend." They had a strange relationship, growling at each other as if they had once been in love or they were going to fall in love. Their disagreements seemed more complex and layered than ideological differences between a Communist and an imperialist missionary. Joseph made overtures to Min-hwan expectantly but Min-hwan always retreated; they were both outsiders in this city. Their friendship was maintained by intelligent sarcasm and jokes about their different worldviews. I felt free and satisfied between the two. We packed lunches and picnicked at Toksugung Palace, Namsan, and the banks of Han River. If I ever stood on the right or the left of our trio, the two gentlemen chivalrously ushered me to the center. My elbows tickled and trembled as I walked, shivering like a rain-soaked kitten, flanked by the two.

Now I wonder if I really did want them both. It's easier to be attracted to one man's despair than it is to desire the love of two men. Ending up with my own loneliness is the easiest and quickest of all. In our triangle, each of us separately felt love and despair and loneliness. I fell for Joseph for the same reason Min-hwan fell for me; the relationship offered an escape from our suffocating reality. Joseph was a welcome respite from the real world, much like a lunchtime picnic that lets you forget about your problems for a few hours.

That was the last year I completely and joyfully experienced the four seasons. After 1949 I always greeted spring flowers, summer downpours, fall sunlight, and winter snow with suspicion and animosity. In September 1948, the People's Republic was established in the northern part of the country. Skirmishes increased at the 38th Parallel and the threat of war hung heavily in the air. But few expected there would actually be a war. Syngman Rhee, the first president of the South Korean government and the first person I would beat up if I could, went around spouting nonsense: "If a war broke out, we would have lunch in Pyongyang and dinner in Sinuiju." Even if you wanted to trust his confidence, the atmosphere was turning more and more savage, and it began to clog our noses and mouths. In 1949, Min-hwan was summoned by the newly established National Rehabilitation and Guidance League, which started an ideological purge that targeted the Communists who seemed antithetical to the South's plans for the country's unification.

He eventually returned grim, humiliated, and damaged. I began to regret not forcing him to go north. "Let's go now," I suggested. "Or to Tokyo. Or America." I was that clueless—no matter where he went, Min-hwan would still have to choose between his wife and his mistress. He no longer needed a daughter figure to share his bed, as he now had an actual, beloved daughter who was endlessly fascinating to him. I shouldn't have tormented him about choosing. If I had truly cared for him, I would have found him a small desk somewhere, where he could sit quietly and translate English poems. But that wasn't a possibility in Korea at the time.

I turned to Joseph for comfort. "What do you think will happen? What will happen to us if the North wins? Min-hwan is acting strangely. He's dark and sad and desperate." Frustrated with my English abilities, I asked him all this in Japanese.

Joseph answered in surprisingly improved Korean. "God will look after this country. Min-hwan is a sensible man. Don't worry."

His banal answer reassured me, and I trusted that his prayers would work. In the meantime, my relationship with Min-hwan was becoming fraught. I couldn't make his anguish and grief dissipate; he was an animal lost in a maze and I was just a younger animal following him and fretting. That was how we gradually took our places as the main characters on the stage of a tragedy. The world around us had already completed its own preparations. Death, killings, and insanity loomed ahead of us. This was three months before the war started.

I don't know how to explain what happened next. Every affair is different, but I didn't know that at the time. I was precocious but I didn't understand the awe-inspiring forces of love. I thought I knew love, though it manifested in different ways for everyone. Joseph was a friend from a different, enchanted world, one I could never be a part of. He was both American and Japanese, as privileged as if he were armed with both a gun and a sword. I envied his freedom, his wealth, his generosity, and felt wronged that I didn't have the things that had never been mine to begin with. I believed myself to be his equal, and to truly be equal to him I needed him to look at me with desire.

"What would possibly happen if you don't pray today?" I asked him one drizzly day.

"Alice, why don't you have any friends?" he asked without answering my question. His gaze was dangerously damp and slippery, like stairs drenched in rain. "You have no one but Min-hwan."

"He's my family, my friend, and my teacher," I protested.

"Only one person in the world can fill that role," Joseph said gently. "A father."

"You don't understand," I said slowly in English. "You never will." Cold air circled my waist; sadness I had suppressed was rising in me. I gazed up at him.

"Alice, I can't betray my friend. That's worse than betraying my faith." His hands were trembling as though he were a priest who had dropped his cross. His palms were damp.

I went to him. We didn't have the will to resist any longer. We held each other, licking and swallowing excuses with our burning tongues. Our desire melted into sticky fluid and seeped into each other. He bucked single-mindedly between my legs and with each thrust something crumbled and crashed within me.

"Alice … oh, Alice …"

That was the day we discovered a new language based on physicality, one that surmounted the communication obstacles between us despite each of our plentiful vocabularies. Our new language was conveyed through warm, tender flesh.

After that, we saw each other several more times, every time hoping it would be the last. And finally, that fateful day arrived. Min-hwan opened the door and stopped in his tracks; his friend and his mistress at the height of pleasure. Moans of climax and a moan of despair filled the room. Min-hwan looked at me icily, his eyes devoid of sympathy, or shared memories, or a future. He turned on his heel and left. Only when Joseph collapsed on top of me did I realize that I knew nothing about this man. I found myself suddenly suspicious: he had been too friendly, his prayers were too eager, and he had fallen too easily into bed with me.

It was too late. Everything warped and collapsed and shattered. I should have acted faster. War was waiting with its maw open, just beyond sight, and I had a sickening hunch I would never see Min-hwan again. I should have taken that feeling more seriously.

After the war, Min-hwan was purged by the North. I heard the news on the day the armistice agreement was signed—July 27, 1953.

The Return of the First Ghost

Evening of February 16, 1954

MY NAME IS ALICE.

"Hello, Joseph."

The man who gave me that name is walking up to me, his pale face emerging from darkness, his jaw as strong and his eyes as sharp as ever. He smiles. Our connection, which was abruptly severed four years ago, bridges that span instantly.

"You're not surprised to see me." Joseph sounds a little disappointed.

I'm not. I never doubted I would see him again. "I was waiting for you. For a long time."

"You're still so …" Joseph catches himself before he says "beautiful." "Alice, you're so thin!" He looks at me with alarm.

"And you're as dashing as ever, Mr. Missionary. God's keeper, am I right?"

He nods, unfazed by my jab.

"Looks like you're not hiding your identity tonight."

Joseph remains calm. "It's cold out here. Let's go inside."

"Are *you* the intelligence officer who's been wanting to question me?"

Joseph goes to the jeep and opens the back door for me. "I'm here as your friend before anything else. I've always been fond of you, Alice."

My supposed friend, with whom I had a passionate affair, is being formal. I try to gather my thoughts. This isn't the Joseph I knew. Well, I guess I never knew him in the first place. I have so many questions for this handsome American intelligence officer who befriended me while pretending to be a missionary. I shouldn't be angry; I vow to be grateful that I can now find out what actually happened.

The jeep speeds through the dark. The wind is forceful. We get out in front of a Quonset hut. It's warm inside. The place is outfitted with an overstuffed couch and a furnace. Joseph sends away the MPs who accompanied us and turns on all the lights. I can tell from his expression that I look even more grotesque under that bluish light.

"Are you here with Marilyn Monroe?" I ask.

He nods noncommittally.

"Why are you here now? You must have heard about me from Hammett."

"I've been in Tokyo this whole time. I've been hearing how you were." Joseph comes over and guides me by the shoulders to the couch. His touch is still light and gentle. "I wanted to come and see you last year when I heard you'd gone to meet Hammett, but I wasn't able to. I'm glad you went to him for help, Alice."

I stare at him. "I remembered your old friend when I got back to Seoul. These days you can't even be a beggar without connections."

"Your English has gotten so good." Joseph smiles.

"Of course it has. I had a great first teacher," I say sarcastically. "You don't have to look at me like that. I know what you really are, so let's stop pretending." I purse my lips and touch my rust-colored hair. "I don't hate you. I know I was the foolish one. I only discovered who you really are quite recently. I found a letter on Hammett's desk with a picture of me inside the envelope, so I knew it was going to you. Everything made sense then. Why you were often wrong about Bible passages, and why you went to Tongnae for business trips—that's where your headquarters were. I realized that when you went to Tokyo for work that last time, it coincided with the Far East headquarters moving to Seoul. Once, I looked in your suitcase and saw photographs with palm trees in them. Now I know that was near Manila, where you were stationed. You weren't that good at your cover, anyway. No missionary would kiss as well as you do. You really were careless. I could have been a spy from the North! What would you have done if I had been?"

Joseph is unruffled. A cool professional. "So why did you go north? Were you abducted?"

I'm caught off guard but recover quickly. "You weren't able to figure it out? That's disappointing. You know the

People's Republic wouldn't leave a top talent like me alone."

Talk of war doesn't sound realistic coming from him. Even if he were in charge of drafting top-secret documents about the war, he's a novice when it comes to what happens on the ground. I turn away as if I don't care. I uncross my legs but my knees are trembling. My hands are shaking, too. I quickly put my hands in my pockets.

"Are you all right?"

"Of course, I'm just coming down with a cold." I try to hide my sudden nervousness, but I know he's already detected it.

He comes to put an arm around me but I shake him off and stand up. My head is momentarily blank at the touch of someone who remembers my body.

"I'm actually here for an important assignment," Joseph says. "When I found out you were the person linked to the incident, I came as soon as I could. We need your help. We'd like to formally request your cooperation. But Hammett told me you're still recovering, so I'm hesitant to make you relive those years."

"Are you?" I retort. "You're really something. How dare you come back years later as though nothing happened between us? Were you laughing at me as you fooled me that whole time?" My anger erupts now, but my pitiful yelling and stomping doesn't even fill the hut.

"I won't insult you with excuses about my behavior," Joseph says earnestly. "Alice, I want you to know this. Nothing was false about our friendship." His beautiful brown eyes seek to reassure me as they had in the past but I'm no longer so naïve.

"If you didn't need something from me you wouldn't be here, apologizing like this. You're sneaky and detached, just like your two sides—Japanese and American." I'm about to continue my attack, but two short American agents with neatly pomaded brown hair walk in.

They stand imperiously before me. Their stony gazes bring me back to my circumstances. Now is not the time to enumerate my many personal grievances. Joseph too quickly assumes a more formal expression and straightens. This isn't the reunion I imagined. A dreary military base isn't an appropriate place for former lovers to meet again. I'm humiliated, standing before my ex-lover as if I'm nothing more than a potential informant. I am just hired help, like a maid or a driver.

The two men give Joseph looks, and he sits me down again, guiding me by my shoulders. "Alice, do you know about radio propaganda? Usually women fluent in the language of the enemy broadcast propaganda to the other side during war. For example during the Second World War, a Japanese woman known as the 'Tokyo Rose' was on Radio Tokyo and was a big hit among American soldiers. The North also broadcast during the Korean War to demoralize American soldiers, and they had an American woman do it. People called her Seoul Crybaby, because she read the list of American casualties in a weepy voice. Maybe she really was crying? It's likely she was forced to do these broadcasts. We didn't know who she was at the time. She somehow sounded both young and old. After the war, we discovered she was a church official and an active missionary in her late thirties. She turned out to be a member of a wealthy East Coast family that had searched for her in vain. We didn't know where she was and she didn't show up during the exchange of POWs, but finally we have located her. She's in Pyongyang. We are making plans to bring her here. But we have a problem with the person who is supposed to help her escape. You know Lim Pok-hun, don't you?"

Seoul Crybaby—what a lovable and pathetic nickname. Seoul is teeming with countless babies who are so sick from hunger and loss that they are no longer able to shed tears.

"What about him?" I ask.

The men study my reaction intently.

Lim takes up very little space in my memory, but he emits a more powerful force than anyone else. I can't believe Lim is the reason Joseph has come back to see me. What an awful bond Lim and I share. The dark, skinny Communist spy with a snake's face and short legs was unlucky enough to be recognized by me on the *Ocean Odyssey* and was caught.

"Wasn't he arrested?"

"No, he escaped as soon as he got to Koje Island and went back north," one of the agents says. "You can't help but be impressed. He stole our field truck and drove over the mountains of Kangwon Province."

Going back north alone as a guerilla—it sounds like something he would do. "What does he have to do with Seoul Crybaby?"

The agents study me warily. "Lim's position in the North became precarious because of his arrest on the ship. He was suspected of being an American spy. So he approached an informant we are working with and proposed that he bring Seoul Crybaby here. In return he demanded safe repatriation to another country and a huge sum of money. But now he's missed several meetings and we can't get in touch with our informant. And nobody knows what Lim looks like."

I feel Joseph glancing at me. "How exactly am I supposed to help you?"

"We need you to describe him to us."

I manage to stifle my laughter. Unbelievable. American spies are supposed to be the best of the best, but sometimes they are pathetically buffoonish—it reminds me of what I heard about brave young Korean country boys, selected from refugee camps and sent to a secret training site run by Americans in Saipan. They were dispatched north for a poorly planned mission and never came back. Perhaps they are still hiding in an underground tunnel in Hamgyong Province awaiting orders, hunting wild rabbits to survive. "I don't remember."

They don't believe me. One of the agents points to the pen and paper on the table. "Can you draw his face?"

The other agent steps forward, his expression growing dangerous.

I look at Joseph, who remains stony-faced. I have no friends here. I begin babbling nervously. "He was a little taller than me, maybe by a couple of inches. He had a sharp nose—like a pen nib. His lips were thin and bluish and—oh, he had a small scar under one eye."

The agent smiles and pushes the paper towards me. "There you go. Just draw what you remember."

Everyone looks at me expectantly, and I have the impression that the pen and paper are equally expectant. I sit down, take the pen, and then boldly draw big diagonal lines on the white paper.

The agents gape at me. Joseph stands up and gives them a look—they're now getting irritated—and sends them out. It's just Joseph and me in the room again. Now that I know what he wants I'm in the position of power. Whether in a game or in love, the one who reveals what he wants always loses. The space between us fills with hostility—all coming from me. I glare at him. He didn't come here to see me. He's here to save some other woman. That idol of the American military is more important to him than me. I now recognize my true emotion towards Joseph: sorrow.

"Alice? Are you all right?"

Tears course down my cheeks. I feel free and unburdened. "I don't draw anymore," I say in Korean.

"You don't have to. We shouldn't have asked you to."

"You knew war was coming. I heard that planes were waiting at the Kimpo Air Base to evacuate Americans. Now we know how you were all cowards. You told us that war wasn't possible, while all the time you were preparing to evacuate and mobilize emergency communications. I mean, I guess Korean politicians and the rich were worse. They hid their yachts off the coast of Pusan and held drunken parties before fleeing to Japan. Only the nameless soldiers and ordinary Koreans were caught in the middle." I am enraged. "I hated you when I discovered who you really were. I thought you could have saved me if you really wanted to. But then I realized it didn't matter. You followed your fate, I followed mine, and Min-hwan followed his. None of it matters. In the end, the only difference is who ends up dead first."

Min-hwan's name flies out of my mouth, ambushing him. We're both startled. We glance at each other furtively, our shared taboo binding us together.

"Now I know why he didn't like you," I continue. "He knew this was who you are. He knew you would interfere with us and run away like a coward."

Joseph stiffens. Everyone has at least one person they have wronged, whose name makes them quake. For both of us it's our romantic Communist—my lover, his friend.

"Did you hear what happened to him?" I ask bitterly. "He vanished. Just like you. I don't know how or when he was abducted by the North, but I heard he was one of the people they purged last year. For being an American imperialist spy." I wipe my tears hastily. I don't want to cry. Complacent tears can't wash away past mistakes.

"He—" Joseph swallows the rest of his words. "I'm sorry," he says instead. "Not a day has gone by that I didn't think about you. I thought you were safe, especially since your uncle worked for the government. When I came back to Seoul that September after UN forces reclaimed the city, I found everything was bombed. I went all the way north to Pyongyang and saw horrible things. The People's Army left piles of corpses in every air raid shelter before retreating. The only thing we took for ourselves were bottles of Vodka left behind in the Soviet embassy. I kept searching for you but all I heard was that you were probably dead. But I knew you would survive somehow." Joseph looks at me sympathetically, benevolently, forgetting who he is. But a gaze, no matter how kind and warm, can't save someone. "Alice—what happened to you?"

That's a really good question, one that I might be asking myself for the rest of my life. Even if I find the answer, I might never cease asking myself. "I don't know. I don't remember all of it. You both disappeared and the People's Army rolled in on Soviet tanks. People ran out into the streets, waving the North Korean flag. I went out to Chongno and saw portraits of Kim Il Sung and Stalin draped on Hwasin department store. It was even worse at the end of the summer. UN forces bombed the city and we heard rumors that they had successfully landed in Inchon and were advancing. I don't remember much after that. I recall being shackled to other people and walking north. They shot you on the spot if you stumbled or couldn't walk straight, so I walked and walked until my feet started bleeding. And then—then I was in a POW camp in Huichon. People called me the crazy girl with gray hair." I'm struggling to catch my breath as the memories flow over me, and Joseph looks alarmed as I cover my face with my hands. I'm like an actress in a tragedy, playing a character created by a famous playwright. The person I'm talking about isn't really me, but an insane woman I am embodying. I can't be myself. That's the only way I can live with myself. I can only exist if I act out all of my truths along with all of the falsehoods.

It's true that some of my memories are fuzzy. I don't remember anything from that autumn. A B-29 bombed my brain and my soul, rendering them into a heap of ash. It was as if napalm rained down one day and incinerated my mind. I kept falling and crying and losing consciousness; my eyes were open but I couldn't see anything. A nun abducted alongside me kept pulling me up and nudging me along. I came to and I was in a prison. I opened my eyes and I was walking. I looked up and I was on a train. Someone whispered that we might be sent to Manchuria with the POWs, but I ended up at a camp with American POWs in Hwichon. I drooled and said nonsensical things. I was tasked with meal preparation and odd jobs. There was no kitchen in that sty, so women in a nearby village cooked at home and brought the food into the camp. I sat in the mud and collected kindling, forgetting I was alive. I didn't dare dream I would survive. One day, I stuck my hands in the furnace, into flames that looked like orange flowers. The woman next to me pulled my hands out in horror. She brought medicinal herbs every day and tended to my burns. As I wandered around, doing my chores, I discovered that she was acting strangely; she would slip something to the American soldiers as she doled out their meals. One day I dashed after her, dove into her skirts, and found small bits of cloth fastened to her undergarments with a pin, designed to slip out easily. The strips were made of thin fabric and printed with instructions to write one's name on in order to prepare for repatriation. They were signed by the commander of the UN forces. She clapped her hand over my mouth in alarm and whispered to me that she had been won over by agents working for the South and was on a secret mission to obtain a list of American POWs to prepare for armistice negotiations and POW exchanges. Even in my delusional state I understood that this could be my opportunity to get out of the camp. I asked her to let me help. She told a South Korean agent about me, and beginning the next day I helped her gather names. The soldiers didn't trust me at first when I cautiously approached them but gradually they began to cooperate. Despite the danger, they wrote down their names. Many were hard to read; some were written with a broken pencil while others were scribbled crookedly, as if under a blanket. Over the course of a month we collected a hundred names. If we had been caught we would have been tortured and shot.

In December we finally received word. I snuck onto a munitions truck in the middle of the night, and rolled off as we rumbled along the mountain roads. When I found my way to the designated village, a southern agent disguised in a People's Army uniform was waiting for me with my co-conspirator and her family. Her husband was suffering from tuberculosis; it looked hopeless for him. Their young granddaughter had lost her parents in a recent bombing, and she stood there, holding her grandmother's hand. That was Chong-nim. The agent hid us in a military truck and drove us to Hamhung, a journey that was fraught with danger. Not long after we arrived, the woman's husband coughed blood into his blanket and lost consciousness. Realizing they couldn't go on she asked me tearfully to take care of Chong-nim. Of course I agreed. She had saved me from the darkest corner of the universe and I would never forget her—although I knew we would never see each other again in this lifetime.

The agent put the child and me on a train to Hungnam. We left at two in the morning and arrived at Hungnam Port three hours later. Already there were a hundred thousand screaming refugees fighting for a place on the boats. US forces were preparing to pull out as the Chinese army pushed south, and we had all heard the rumor that America was going to detonate a nuclear bomb over Hungnam. The desperate clamor of the refugees shook the sky and the earth and the ocean. The dark hair of all those people, stretching to the horizon, made my heart pound. I didn't have the will or the confidence to shove through them; my knees gave way and I sank to the ground. Everything began to grow faint. I was more afraid of the ferocious will of the masses than I was of the bombers flying above our heads. I couldn't breathe. My eyes rolled up into my skull. Chong-nim dribbled water from our canteen into my mouth and massaged my frozen legs with her tiny hands, blowing on them, trying to warm me up.

The 1st Division of the American Navy had already left Hungnam and was on its way to Pusan. When the transport ships to evacuate the military began arriving, the terror of the refugees on the wharf surged. People didn't sleep or eat as they waited anxiously for the soldiers to board the ships. Cattle yoked to carts were bellowing, infants were wailing, and a weeping father was using his few words of English to show American soldiers his Bible as proof that he was not a Communist, begging them to take his family along. Finally, civilians were allowed to board. People shoved and leaped into the cold water to get on the ships. A couple holding hands were split apart by the crowd; siblings who had lost their parents wailed in terror; and an old man who had given up trying to get onboard was waving to his son on the deck, exchanging final goodbyes. People threw their precious belongings into the water to reduce the weight of the ship. Sewing machines, vanities, violins, puppies, and ceramic vases floated in the water. Nobody was going to help us; we were just a crazy woman and a tiny girl. Each ship was so crammed with people that it was a miracle they were still afloat. We were nearly trampled to death as we tried to get in a line. We could feel the Chinese army advancing on us. The US Navy planes that had taken off from the aircraft carriers dropped bombs; it was as if they were planning to leave all their shells in Hungnam. From time to time I felt silence, as if my ears were stunned by the explosions and had fallen off my head. The smell of the burning city paralyzed me. Chong-nim gripped onto my hand, trying her best not to cry. Her small hand was drenched, as if she were crying through her palms. I looked around, befuddled, and saw some American soldiers stoking a fire as they waited to get on a ship. They were burning a heaping mound of food and munitions that wouldn't fit onboard. I dragged Chong-nim over. Help us, she has to live, I babbled in English. This girl has to live. They stared at me before opening a can of tomato soup and giving it to us. Calm down, they said. I worked in the American military government, I went on. I have American friends. A redheaded soldier listened sympathetically before heaving Chong-nim on his back. Follow me, he said. A new cargo ship had entered the wharf and was being moored. People were swarming towards it, but our new friend took a different route and ran towards the middle of the ship. He shouted up at the men on deck and asked them to let us on. They quickly let down a net and the soldier climbed it like a ladder, Chong-nim on his back and pulling me along. My legs quaked and my palms burned but I climbed as if my life depended on it. Once we got onto the deck the soldier rummaged in his pockets and took out a Hershey's bar. He handed it to us and scrambled back down the net. I called out my thanks and asked his name. He just smiled and said, Bon voyage. He saluted and went off. That ship was the *Ocean Odyssey*. The crew ran around, talking in worried tones. The ship's maximum capacity was sixty people and there were no weapons on board. A sailor gestured for us to go down the ramp to the cargo bay. In English, I desperately told him that we needed fresh air because of illness. He let us stay and went towards the gangway. Soon people began swarming onto the ship. The crew hid their concerns and sent the refugees down to the cargo bays. Even though they couldn't communicate, everyone followed the crew's orders. The ship was filled from the bottom, from the fifth to the fourth to the third to the second levels. People found spots in the narrow passageways. Only the deck was left but there were still so many people on the gangway. I didn't think the ship would ever leave. I would end up as a pile of ash, along with the supplies burning on the beach.

But the captain and the crew continued to load people onto the ship with a sense of mission, as if they were Noah's descendants. A ship that wasn't supposed to carry even a hundred passengers ended up filled with thousands. It took all day just to get everyone onboard. Night fell. Chong-nim and I watched as bombers embroidered the sky, and fire and smoke enveloped the dying city. Families with bundles dangling from them were on the deck with us, quietly praying for survival. Hope propelled the ship forward. The *Ocean Odyssey* left for Pusan, escorted by the 3rd Division of the US Navy, which guarded Hungnam to the end. I knew it was very possible that we would be blasted by one of the mines blanketing the waters of Hungnam. Perhaps something worse would have happened had I not spotted Lim Pok-hun on the deck among the laborers. I'd only spoken to the North Korean agent once in Seoul, when he approached me in the Art Association to comment on my drawings of Stalin. But I knew that face. I remembered his quiet, meticulous words, and the way they had sent a shiver down my spine. There had been rumors that North Korean spies were disguised as civilians and were moving among refugees, plotting attacks, and so male refugees were under constant scrutiny. Yet Lim had somehow made it onto the ship. I grabbed a crew member as he passed by and whispered, "That man over there, he isn't a civilian." The crew quickly grabbed him and dragged him to the captain's cabin. I had to go with them to give them my statement. Our eyes met for a moment and he revealed his white teeth and smiled. He eventually gave up resisting when his various IDs were discovered hidden in his clothes. He was tied up and watched closely in the cabin for the rest of the journey.

The wind grew stronger as we entered the East Sea; fear and hunger reached a peak. Sailors gave out water and cans of food and even the gum from their pockets but none of it was enough to fill all of those bellies. People who ended up sitting down weren't able to stand back up because of the crowd; they had to soil themselves where they sat. Many hadn't had a sip of water in three days.

Death danced with wide-open jaws just beyond the ship. But life was persistent. On our first day in the East Sea, a child was born in the nurse's cabin. Two additional miracle babies were born before we finally entered Pusan harbor on Christmas Eve. But Pusan was overflowing with refugees and we weren't allowed to dock. We were instead sent to Koje Island. I couldn't believe I was back in the South. Chong-nim, gripping my hand, looked out at the blue sea, her eyes sparkling. Heat radiated from her frozen blue cheeks. I would have given up trying to return if it hadn't been for her. I took out my most precious treasure, the Citizen watch with his initials, Y.M.H., engraved on it. I gave it to Chong-nim and said, don't ever lose this. If someone tries to take it from you, you scream as loudly as you can. Chong-nim tied it to the inside of her blouse, nodding. The broadcast system began to play Christmas carols, and I started to cry. I had survived. Misery was my fate but life was still beautiful; my fate was just part of my life. The war hadn't destroyed everything. War had killed the love and hope and warmth within me, but it had also spared me. I covered my face with my hands, sobbing out the last bit of love to shore up the life remaining inside. I wiped away my tears and looked at my hands, those malicious hands that had killed the thing most precious to the man I loved.

Joseph holds both of my hands. I ball them into fists. I don't want him to see the red scars beneath my black lace gloves.

"Alice," he says gently, "I had no idea what you went through."

Now I'm the one who's calm. I feel better, even though I haven't told him everything.

"Did you find your mother? She lived in the North, didn't she?"

"She passed away," I reply, my face stony.

"I see. I'm sorry." Joseph sounds sad. He thinks my mother died during the war.

In fact she died before the war broke out. When I learned this my heart shattered, but I later decided it was better that way; at least she didn't have to live through the war. I cried and buried her in my heart.

"I was surprised by your countrymen," Joseph says. "They were studying in makeshift tent schools, making roofs out of powdered-milk cans that they pounded straight. Everyone had such a strong will to live, from the youngest to the oldest. It wouldn't have been easy to live through that all by yourself. Why didn't you ask your uncle for help?"

"He was ashamed of me. Some people didn't lose a thing during the war, and those people don't understand anything. But others did help. The woman I board with—I met her on Koje Island. My friend who's a nurse—I met her in Pusan and lived with her for a while. And of course, if Hammett hadn't given me a job, I might have had to sell my body to survive."

Joseph looks at me with concern. "And ... the girl?"

"I—I lost her. At the camp. It was too chaotic. It's all my fault. I didn't realize I could lose a child that easily." I search around for excuses.

Joseph places my hands gently in my lap, one on top of the other. "Don't, Alice. Don't do that. Remember you have more people on your side than you think."

Damn. Does he know that I tried to end my life? I must have underestimated his talents for gathering information. He embraces me as if he knows. I turn my head to the side, rejecting his kindness. I haven't been fully honest with him yet. I don't deserve such sympathy. "Is that so? It's nice of you to say that," I say snidely. "Don't worry, I won't think of you as one of those many people who care about me."

Joseph frowns. His eyes, the color of black tea, tremor slightly. What is he thinking? "That girl Chong-nim—you said she could be in an orphanage in Pohang?"

"Yes."

"Let me help you find her."

"Really? Would you?"

Joseph nods. "I'll see what I can find out. I'll let you know tomorrow afternoon."

"Thank you!" I leap up and kiss him on the cheek. I'm surprised by how rough it is. I step back.

We both blush. More than anything, we are surprised by the other's coolness. Were we always so detached? We both quickly hide our disappointment. Was our passionate affair four years ago such an obvious mistake? We look sadly and embarrassedly at each other. Perhaps we could have become true lovers if we'd met in a different time and place. Even though we thought we had loved each other, "we" never existed; everything had been based on falsehoods. Any emotion, even if it had been real, doesn't matter now. We fold up that foolish, innocent time and store it in our hearts. If we take out that memory on a gray afternoon in the future we would feel embarrassed but would perhaps feel less lonely. After all, the memory of a betrayal is still a memory.

A Living Ghost

February 17, 1954

"DID YOU SLEEP WELL, MARILYN?" I OPEN THE DOOR TO her room, which is pungent with Chanel perfume.

She is disheveled, in pale blue pajamas—perhaps silk—and a fur coat. Fuzzy green slippers are on her feet. I'm disappointed. I glimpse crystal glasses and Lucky Strikes strewn on the floor around her bed. I'm concerned she might have taken cold medicine in addition to the pills I gave her yesterday.

"My face is always puffy in the morning," she tells me. "You look like you haven't slept a wink yourself."

Women with anxious nerves recognize each other.

"I met an old friend last night," I explain.

"Oh, I see."

"Perhaps I'll see him again tonight. I'm looking for a little girl, and the orphanage she's supposed to be at is near here."

Marilyn purses her lips and shows interest. "An orphan girl?"

"Yes, I came to know her during the war. She's the granddaughter of the woman who saved my life."

"I do hope you find her and take her from the orphanage. I spent some time in one myself when I was a girl. I was very lonely." Marilyn picks up a Zippo lighter from the floor.

I remember reading about her unhappy childhood.

"The only good thing about the orphanage was that I could see the studio where my mother worked from the window." Marilyn slides her first cigarette of the day between her lips, embodying regret and pleasure. She is able to talk about her misfortune calmly. She was once a sad girl and now is the most beloved woman in the world. Without her beauty this transformation might not have been possible. A woman's beauty is powerful enough to change her fate, though it becomes useless as she grows old.

"You're scheduled for a special photo shoot this morning." I hand her a baseball jacket and cap. "Here, this should fit you." Today's schedule begins with a commemorative photo with Korean baseball players. It was my idea; it would be a perfect photo for a magazine cover.

I head to the field first. Two Korean players are waiting for her in clean striped uniforms with their team's name on them: *Golden Dragons*. I tell them Miss Monroe isn't feeling well and ask for their cooperation, but they don't seem all that enthused. Maybe they're not fans of hers. We wait for a long time, shivering in the cold, and members of the press begin to grumble. It seems she's notorious for tardiness. I think about her complicated expression last night, the way she was intoxicated by her own reflection in the mirror. A woman in front of a mirror always hesitates, unsure of her own beauty. Maybe Marilyn is more concerned about that than the rest of us precisely because she is so stunning. You can't enjoy anything lesser once you've tasted the real thing. Since she knows the peak of beauty, she might always be yearning for it.

She finally appears on the field and everyone suppresses their annoyance. She walks towards us, swinging her baseball cap mischievously. She must have needed all this time to conceal her sickly aura with makeup. Somehow her bright smile looks pitiful. How long has she spent alone in front of a mirror, learning how to paint her face so beautifully? I wonder how much time she spends taking off her makeup. Does she wipe her lipstick off while avoiding her own tired, lonely reflection, the way other women do?

I introduce Park and Kim, the baseball players, and Marilyn shakes hands with them happily and links her arms through theirs. She takes the bat, ready to hit. Lights flash and pop. I ask the officer watching from the sidelines about Joe DiMaggio.

"He's the best right-handed batter ever," he exults. "That Yankee Clipper has a phenomenal swing."

I imagine Joe DiMaggio as a majestic sailboat, a man fated to embark on a lonely voyage. Marilyn is smiling, the bat resting on her shoulder. What is it like to have a husband? What is it like to have as your protector a man who is like a sailboat or a tank or a bomber?

"He's the best player in the world," the officer continues. "It's too bad we can't watch him play anymore."

"Oh, he doesn't play anymore?"

"No. He retired."

"What does he do now?"

The officer nods at Marilyn. "Now he's Mr. Marilyn Monroe."

Marilyn holds the bat and twists, wobbling adorably like a boat without an oar. She doesn't seem all that familiar with the game of baseball. She manages to graze the ball with her bat and it floats for a moment before falling to the ground and rolling towards me. I pick it up and slide it into my pocket.

"Have you always liked baseball?" I ask her after she's done.

She pauses before confessing, "No, I didn't even know Joe was a baseball player. What about you? Do you like baseball?"

"I used to go to games with my friends. I actually went to watch a game on the day the war broke out four years ago."

It was Sunday, June 25, 1950, and I was headed to Tongdaemun Stadium for a game. I would have gone with Joseph and Min-hwan had our friendship continued, but I was alone that day. I eventually left and plodded home. On the streetcar people whispered that battles had broken out near the 38th Parallel. As we neared

Chungjongno, I saw Yonhap Sinmun's extra that the Korean Army had fought off the People's Army in northern Kyonggi Province. Even so, it just seemed like the beginning of summer. I didn't realize the war had begun, or that the time of farewell had drawn near.

"I understand Americans love baseball," I say.

"Yes, that's true. Hollywood stars aren't the only stars we have," Marilyn says.

"I still don't understand what's so interesting about that game," I tell her.

Marilyn crinkles her nose and nods. "Me neither, to be honest." She takes off her cap and fluffs up her blonde hair. Her golden helmet glints in the sunlight. "The baseball diamond is clearly not a girl's best friend." She winks and I laugh.

In the afternoon, people grow impatient as they clamor for Marilyn, so we barely manage to eat lunch before we are ordered to the next stop. A helicopter is already waiting at the airport to take us to the marine camp in Pohang. Hammett waves me over to the aircraft. We can't hear each other over the roar of the engine and the wind from the blades. He asks how the visit with Joseph went.

I just smile.

"He's on assignment, but he did want to see you, Alice. Give him a break." Hammett seems a bit wary now that he knows I am aware of Joseph's real identity.

I don't really care. I just hope Joseph will find Chongnim. "Yes, it was great to see him again. He told me he'd get me a wonderful present, too."

In the last few years I have given up on my life. Looking for Chong-nim is the least I can do. Perhaps I'm doing it for myself; maybe I could believe in myself again if the child who believed in me is by my side.

We arrive in Pohang and it's a similar situation as our last stop. Hundreds of soldiers are here to see her. Marilyn is waving from the top of a tank as it circles the camp, more authoritative than the commander of the UN forces. The soldiers let out a thunderous cheer. A marine with a camera is sprinting after her as if he is a movie director. He stumbles and rolls in the dirt. They are all behaving as if none of them has a girlfriend back home. If their girlfriends came here and saw them, they would set everything on fire, enraged by their betrayal. Excited soldiers pack the area from the outdoor stage all the way to the bottom of the hill. Their stomping shakes the ground and their wolf whistles leave my ears ringing. The band and singers warm up as Marilyn gets ready in the dressing room backstage. She takes off her bolero to reveal bluish goosebumps on her shoulders and arms; she's wearing only a silk dress.

Betty feels her forehead and shakes her head. "She's going to catch pneumonia!" she shouts.

Everyone freezes. Of course, it's out of concern for Marilyn, but everyone is more worried about what might happen if she doesn't go onstage. Marilyn gets up cheerfully, but her shoe strap snaps off. Everyone stares at her bare foot, mortified, as if it's her nude body. People begin rushing around to find replacement shoes. The performers' feet are too big and the women in uniform are all wearing muddy boots.

"Take them off, Alice!" Betty pushes me into a chair and rips my shoes off. My navy blue shoes from relief supplies flown in from the West. She shoves them onto Marilyn's feet. I flush.

"I can tap in these," Marilyn says, trying them out.

Thankfully they go somewhat with her dress. I am suddenly barefoot and the one person who is displeased; somehow, a star with diamonds as her best friend has taken my only pair of shoes. I'm annoyed by them all. They're the ones who gave us the relief goods in the first place and now they're snatching them away. If I'm being honest with myself, I'm embarrassed that my worn stockings are on view.

On the bandmaster's cue, Marilyn runs onstage. I follow her, my feet cold and bare. I peek from behind the stage curtains as if I'm a child watching my first circus. The marines lose their minds. It's as if they are seeing their guardian angel, the goddess of the ocean. A soldier hands over a giant poster of her and she autographs her own face. She says hello to the audience, and her innocent and seductive voice moves thousands of men. She begins singing, her voice as sweet and warm as cocoa. I watch with admiration as she embraces the world. I swing my hips like she does, and try to follow the drummer's beat. Roars of ecstasy slap the bottoms of my feet. As she embraces the sky and the wind, the music and the men, I am inspired. I want to be as alive as she is, living my life with physicality.

I want to be deafened by applause I will remember forever. I want to look down at the men who dream of sleeping with me. None of that is possible, of course. These things are possible only for actresses, and that is why God has created them. From behind the stage I watch as Marilyn stands alone in front of over ten thousand pining men. She is white and pure, like a lamb at an altar. Actually, she is a cunning sheep, having gone willingly up to that altar and enjoying her own sacrifice. Men drool but she is the one who is actually satiated. She is no mere woman; she is an actress, smiling the most beautiful smile and stealing your soul. But what I really want is what an actress can never have—hope. I want love from just one man, the kind of love that takes over one's soul. Maybe I'm being harsh, but I think this would be impossible for an actress whose value resides in being everyone's object of desire. I watch Marilyn dance. Her star, though alone and far from the rest of us, shines so brightly that it hurts my eyes.

After the performance and a visit to the barracks, Marilyn finally collapses. Everyone is relieved; she will now be able to rest. Her room is in a nearby officer dorm. Handsome Army doctors are lining up in an effort to treat her and a short man from the studio is busily turning away reporters.

A houseboy tugs on my skirt. "Excuse me. Is Miss Monroe's hair really blonde? I heard it could be fake." He continues to ask silly questions even though I rap him on the head with my knuckles for his foolishness. I tell him she is married but he weepily refuses to believe me.

I manage to shoo him away and go inside. Betty and another nurse officer are with her. For some reason, after having beheld Marilyn surrounded by men, seeing her among women feels unfamiliar to me. Exhausted, she is leaning sideways on the couch. Half of her makeup is washed off; her face is half-blank. I can't believe this tired woman is *the* Marilyn Monroe. I relate my encounter with the houseboy and everyone laughs except for her.

"They are so smart, those boys. They don't know the alphabet but they speak English so fluently," Betty says with genuine admiration.

"How did he know my color is fake?" Marilyn asks in a husky voice.

I stare at her in shock, and she tells me calmly that she is actually a redhead. I want to tell her that my hair isn't naturally wiry and strange like this, but I don't.

Betty jumps in to say knowingly that they use electric shock to bleach hair in Hollywood.

"But now this is my real color," Marilyn murmurs, sipping water with effort. "If Marilyn Monroe isn't a blonde, everyone is going to feel betrayed."

I catch myself scrutinizing her hair as if I were tasked with detecting fake jewels. I grow embarrassed and turn away.

Marilyn closes her eyes, her expression troubled and lonely. Maybe it's not just exhaustion and a cold. Perhaps she's realized she is all alone in a strange country. She might be realizing that she has to go to sleep alone tonight though she is still ostensibly on her honeymoon. No amount of medication will help her sleep soundly when she is missing her husband.

Captain Walker knocks and comes in to check on Marilyn. He conveys a rambling wish for her to feel better and cocks his head at me to follow him. Outside, he tells me that her health is the Information Service's responsibility—hence mine. He is about to go on but thankfully an MP comes over to tell me that someone is looking for me.

Joseph. He's back. With news of Chong-nim. Or with her. I dash outside. He's waiting there, just like last night, the black car idling behind him in the fog. Yellow headlights illuminate his waist.

"Joseph!" I call.

He turns his head. Only half of his face is visible. It crumples, partly ravaged by the darkness. "Alice." He pauses. Is his voice trembling?

I can tell something has happened. "Did you find her? Did you find Chong-nim?"

Joseph comes closer and lets out a sigh. He smells like cigarettes. "Alice, you're going to be shocked by this. I wanted to tell you yesterday, but he hadn't made his mind up yet."

My nervous face is reflected in his eyes.

"But I think it's time." He steps back and opens the rear door of the car. He beckons for me to get in. His forehead is red, tense.

I go towards the car, my heart pounding. I'm overpowered by the smell of cigarettes coming from inside.

Something dark is in the back seat. It's not a child or a woman. He leans towards me, dipping his face into the light.

A short scream pierces my eardrums. Mine. I fall. Joseph grabs me before I faint. I see the man get out of the car.

Yo Min-hwan.

I close my eyes.

This has to be a dream, although dreams you recognize as such are almost always nightmares. A girl walks through Seoul before its destruction, arm in arm with two men, who laugh at her jokes and sugar her coffee and discuss her drawings. *This is love*, she thinks. She goes to palaces and to cafés and to art exhibitions with them. But one of them is already feeling disillusioned. The girl is bored with the affair and desires the secret she shares with the other man. Their secret is discovered by the disillusioned man in a dramatic, vulgar way, enabling him to treat her with scorn. But he refuses to do that, making her even lonelier and eternally guilty. One day, he disappears like the wind, and war creeps towards the city he's left behind.

I open my eyes. What is going on? I close them again. I can't believe what is happening. Joseph and Min-hwan are watching over me and I am lying on a bed.

"Ae-sun, can you sit up?"

Am I really hearing that low, kind voice? I open my eyes to look at him. He has attempted to disguise himself with horn-rimmed glasses and his hair combed forward, but his cold, clear eyes, reminiscent of stones in a creek, can't be covered up.

"He's not a ghost, Alice," Joseph says.

Of course. He can't be a ghost. A ghost wouldn't smell like an ashtray. How am I supposed to accept what is going on? He was dead. But now he's here, right before my eyes. "Why are you doing this to me?" Even though I know the world operates according to secret agreements beyond my understanding, this is absurd.

"I'm sorry. We had to be careful." Joseph hands me a cup of water, contrite.

I push their hands away and sit up. I must be in a guesthouse at the camp. The room has a bed and a desk and a coat hook, and it smells musty. The fire in the fire-place was so hastily made that the flames are wild; even the inside of my mouth feels hot. The window is black, as if covered by dark paper. It's like the stage set of a one-act play by an amateur theater group. Even the ink bottle on the desk looks like a prop; if I bow I might hear a smattering of applause.

I look at Min-hwan. "I heard you died up north. That's what we all thought."

"That's no rumor. I am dead. I'll be a dead man until I'm really dead for good." Min-hwan spouts nonsense calmly.

I turn to Joseph for help. "If this isn't a dream, I need you two to be honest with me. This is cruel. Are you trying to give me a heart attack? Speak!"

"Calm down, Alice," Joseph says in hesitant Korean. "He was in Tokyo with me."

I turn to Min-hwan angrily. "Didn't I ruin your friendship with Joseph? Since when are you best friends again? Did you know about Joseph from the beginning? Am I the only one who was fooled?"

An awkward silence. I am now suspicious of everything. How did an American intelligence officer become friends with an official of the Workers' Party of South Korea? "Were you—are you an American spy?" I ask Min-hwan, my voice trembling.

He looks at me, frowning, neither confirming nor denying.

I pick out the confused questions swimming in my head, one by one. "Both of you disappeared without any explanation. So why don't you explain yourselves now?"

Min-hwan is chillingly calm. "I went back home to my parents' village. I was there when the war began. War becomes mixed up with individual resentments in a small rural community—kids wearing armbands were running around. It makes you wonder if humans have really evolved. My parents, my siblings, and their families were all killed because of my brother's job as police chief. I survived because one of the servants hid me in a cave in the hills. His wife secretly brought me leftover rice and I lived like a wild rat. I came back to Seoul but I couldn't find you. I couldn't find anyone. I floated around like a ghost. Joseph brought me to Tokyo, and I vowed never to return. But then I heard that you were alive so I had to come back."

I look at his delicate, dignified lips, those lips that used to read Ibsen plays to me. Now his mouth seems desiccated, nothing more than a breathing hole. His lips hardly move as he stoically conveys the bare minimum of information. Perhaps he is afraid of reawakening the sorrow and pain he's managed to quiet. Perhaps he fears he will end up banging his head against the wall in order to drown out those emotions, before cynically accepting that his small share of sadness and pain does not merit such a dramatic reaction. From the wide viewpoint of the universe, the fate of a man is no different from the fate of an ant. That's something everyone needs to be mindful of. I look sympathetically at his lips as though to reverently kiss his hardships away. I want to hold and soothe him, but I don't forget that we are in a truce. If I want to, I can drop a bomb and burn him to a crisp.

"You don't seem happy to see me again," Min-hwan says, disappointed.

"No, I am happy. No matter what, being alive is a blessing." I can't wait any longer. I finally loosen my hold on the dangerous question that has been strangling me. "And your wife and daughter?" I turn nonchalantly and look at Min-hwan's reflection in the glass.

His lips tremble.

"They're missing," Joseph cuts in. "By the time he went home his wife and daughter had gone to her family's home in Hongsong. He went there right away but they never arrived. He thought they must have crossed paths so he went back home again, but they weren't there. As he went from relative's house to relative's house, the war began."

I try to figure out what kind of expression I should be wearing. Joseph catches my eye. He is studying me with his sharp investigator's gaze. I become flustered.

"Oh, I see …" I sound suspicious even to myself.

"My in-laws' house was bombed," Min-hwan explains. "I don't think anyone was able to escape. I'm just one of the many people who lost their family during the war."

My heart begins to pound. I turn my back and head to the fireplace. "I'm jealous you were able to leave this place." I try to tame my shaky voice.

"Come with me." Min-hwan stands behind me and puts his hands on my shoulders. "Let's forget about what happened and start over somewhere new. Whether it's Japan or America or Berlin. We can go wherever you want." His glasses reflect the flames in the fireplace. It's as if red tears are pooling in his eyes.

"You must have forgotten how we parted," I remind him. "You didn't forgive me then and you never will."

Joseph looks away, embarrassed.

Min-hwan comes closer to me, his expression resolutely blank. "I've forgotten everything. You should, too. That's the only way we can go on. You don't need my forgiveness, since I don't even remember what happened." He embraces me, his impatience twining around me. I'm paralyzed by his desperate hope.

"And there's good news," he continues, barely able to contain his excitement. "I might be able to find Song-ha."

"What? Your daughter?" Stunned, I lean back to look at him.

"I've been searching for her for years, and I have finally heard about a girl who fits her description. We're going to an orphanage near Suyuri, in Seoul, to see her. Come with us."

I back away slowly, watching this poor man, hanging all the happiness of the rest of his life on this one impossible hope. What can I do for him? All I can do is to help him maintain this hope for one more night. "All right. Let's." I turn to Joseph, "Can Min-hwan and I stay here tonight, together?"

Joseph searches my face, instantly suspicious of my intentions.

I disarm him with an arch joke. "It would be scandalous if the three of us were to spend the night together, wouldn't it?"

His face momentarily betrays his embarrassment, but then Joseph reassumes his kind expression and spreads his arms to indicate that he will step aside for my original lover to take his place by my side. "Alice, walk me to the door, won't you?"

When I approach, he whispers, "I went to the orphanage today but I couldn't find Chong-nim. I'm sorry."

Disappointment blooms in my chest. That orphanage had been my last hope.

"Alice," Joseph says suspiciously. "Are you hiding something from me?"

I step backward, away from his probing gaze. "That's a question I should ask you, isn't it? Who else are you going to bring back from the dead?"

"I'm sorry. But Alice ..."

"Look, I'm still recovering from seeing Min-hwan again. I need some time." I smile tightly and push him along.

"Did you put an ad in the paper, trying to trace a child? Last year? What's this about a watch? You didn't tell me that."

"Thanks for checking the orphanage," I say. "Let's talk tomorrow."

He studies me suspiciously as the door closes. I turn away. I don't know what he thinks I'm up to, but I don't want to tell him everything just yet. At least not tonight.

The two of us are alone at last. We look at each other with resignation and despair. Together we are like an old pine tree, standing alone, surrounded by a forest fire, waiting for its ultimate demise.

"Are you a ghost?" I ask, and it's not in jest. There is so much I do not know about this man, who has survived by adopting the life of a stranger. In some ways his existence is more outlandish and more cowardly than mine.

"I'm a ghost floating around the back alleys of Tokyo. It hasn't been that hard, actually. Nobody has looked for me as hard as I thought they might."

"You really hated this place that much?"

"In the end I didn't even have the energy to feel sympathy." With a slightly bewildered air, he approaches and strokes my hair. To me, everything about him is sad, but he seems only to be bothered by my hair. "What happened?" he asks.

"I grew old. I guess I couldn't wait until I was actually old." I take his hand from the top of my head and lead him to the bed. I lay him down. He curls up like a baby bird in its egg. I lie down, my back against his chest. We listen to each other's breathing with nervousness, as if we are siblings about to commit incest. I reach back and place his hand on my stomach. His scent, which had perfumed his pillow years ago, tickles my nose. It's been a long time. He keeps touching my hair, stroking my parting with the experienced hand of an old lover. His thin finger traces the path on my head before pausing. It feels the way it used to; his touch and smell yank me back to the past. Are we in the past or in the present? Is it possible for us to pretend that war hasn't penetrated and damaged our souls? That the corpses we saw in the streets could have been pieces of wood that had fallen from the sky? That the horrible rumor about a female partisan caught and raped in Chiri Mountain, her breasts, tongue, and reproductive organs cut out before being discarded, might just be a horrible fairytale from a country far away? We can enjoy the romance of this dramatic reunion if we tell ourselves that we are the same as we were before.

"How has life been in Tokyo?" I ask.

His damp sigh tickles my earlobe. "Pathetic."

"What have you been doing?"

"Making flyers."

I laugh.

"It's true. After 1951 the AFIED didn't make flyers, the UN forces did. They would be printed in Tokyo and flown over here in a B-29 to be distributed. I translated them into Korean. They were about how the UN forces are working hard to achieve peace for the Korean people, how many young men from the North are being shot because the armistice is being delayed, that kind of thing. You probably saw a few I edited myself."

"I shouldn't have thrown them out, then," I tease. "I have strong opinions on propaganda. When you came back to Seoul, did you see any People's Army posters? Some of them were mine. Nobody drew Stalin as well as I did."

"I must have seen your work, then," he says.

We laugh. When you face a brutal reality, all you can do is make jokes. I smile bitterly, glad that we can't see each other's expression right now.

He strokes my hand. "What's this? Did you get hurt?" He pokes through a hole in my glove to touch the scar on my palm. "Your hand—and you're an artist."

"I'm fine now." I don't shake him off. Instead, I take off my gloves and put my hand in his. "Do you remember the last time we saw each other?"

He lets out a heavy sigh.

"You said that I should be ashamed."

"Please don't dwell on the pain I caused you."

"No, you were right. I had to learn how to feel shame. It was arrogant to think I was born with it." I want him to say he can't forgive me and to push me away, but he keeps holding me silently, embracing the cause of his most humiliating moment. His effort to forget how I rolled around naked with another man scares me. It makes me sad. I can't accept who he's become. He's just one of many people for whom oblivion has become the criterion for survival. And I'm the one who pushed him into his dark loneliness.

"Thank you for being alive," he whispers. "Maybe I'll get to see Song-ha tomorrow." His voice breaks my heart. I carefully file it away in my memories. I'll take it out tomorrow as I meet my death.

A Letter

May 1950

I STOMPED AROUND THE ROOM, UNABLE TO TAME MY rage. My hair was tangled and soaked in tears; I looked like a tsunami survivor wearing seaweed on my head. I banged my head on the wall and bit my fingernails and wailed. But inside I felt numb. I knew that this paltry show of emotion wouldn't draw out his sympathy.

"You should have some shame." That was all Min-hwan said when I dragged myself to his house to apologize, before he slammed the door behind me.

I waited all day long outside his boarding house, anticipating his hatred and scorn, but I couldn't hear anything from inside. His stony silence set fire to my instincts. With my gambler's disposition, courtesy of my father, I staked everything on this hand, even though I could sense I would lose. All of my emotions, my love, my hate, my sympathy, my reverence—all of it gushed out. Knowing I wouldn't be forgiven for this transgression, I acted in desperation.

Min-hwan refused to even look at me. To him I was merely a stone or a wall or smoke. It wasn't our demise I couldn't stand; it was his demeanor. I was the one who betrayed him but somehow it was as if he had been waiting for this particular ending all along.

Joseph came to see me a few times in my uncle's house, surprisingly calm and detached, as if nothing had changed. "It might be this way because this is the only way it can be," he said. He didn't seem to be in love with me, but he didn't seem regretful, either.

"Stop coming by! We can't see each other anymore!" I shuddered, not out of dislike but because I had to stop myself from hanging on to him.

Because that was what I wanted to do—lean on him. Of course I imagined fleeing with him; I had an active imagination. But I was afraid. I was scared that I would learn his true feelings for me. Maybe I was only the object of his desire while he was stuck in a foreign land. My fragile, foolish heart was longing for love. We had shared something, hadn't we? We had to be partners in crime, otherwise what was the point of it all? But was it even possible to have a relationship when you were always listening for footsteps outside the door and having to ignore your feelings of guilt every time? What kind of man loves a mistress who can betray her married lover? Even if he did I would have rejected him as an idiot.

Joseph came to see me one spring night. I had been avoiding him in a petty spirit of revenge and to protect my self-respect. He was different that night; he wasn't anxious, trying to soothe my despair. He stared at me coolly, but his tone was heartfelt. "Alice, if I hold out my hand will you accept it?"

I felt a pang of relief but shook my head.

"Do you think Min-hwan deserves to be pined over like this?" His words clawed at me. He looked at me with a suddenly unfamiliar expression.

"Just leave," I said. "It doesn't matter to you. Stop getting involved."

"He's your past. You can only be free when he's not around. I'm going to ask one last time. Are you still waiting for him, despite all of this?"

The heady smell of locust flowers floated in through the open window. I wanted to surrender to that suffocating sweetness. Instead, I stood and turned my back on him.

"That's too bad," Joseph said. "He isn't worth it." He turned and left, slamming the door.

The flowery scent followed him out. I wanted to run after him but I couldn't move. Joseph didn't come by after that night. Alone, I shriveled in Min-hwan's silence. I thought I would go mad. I was still young and naïve. So I plotted a crude act of vengeance, typical of someone who was no longer rational. It was something only a rejected mistress could possibly think of. I wrote a letter and sent it to his family home.

Dear Mrs. Chong Ha-ryon,

I apologize for introducing myself like this. My name is Kim Ae-sun, your husband's longtime live-in lover. We've never met, but I presume you have known about me. I'm sure you suspected something or heard rumors. I won't go into our situation here. In short, we would like to officially wed. Since this is impossible without your cooperation and understanding, I am writing to ask you for your assent before we ask for permission from his parents. I know this letter must be shocking and unpleasant, but I cannot continue to sit on the side with such patience and understanding. Please free him from your hypocritical marriage …

I ran to the Central Post Office and mailed the mean-spirited letter, intended purely to make life difficult for Min-hwan, to shake him from his moral high ground, not understanding the destruction it would unleash.

Seoul Crybaby
February 18, 1954

THE LAST DAY OF MY LIFE BEGINS WITH BEAUTY. I WAKE up and find a note on my pillow.

Going to find Song-ha with Joseph. See you in Seoul.

I rip the note to shreds. The white paper pieces flutter limply to the floor. He won't find his daughter. He won't see me again. I think about his hopeful, expectant face. That hope will shatter and stab him in the heart. He will flail, confused, grasping at his spurting heart, and fall. I can't bear to watch that happen. That's why I've made my decision. I can't face him. I choose instead to vanish from this world.

I go to the desk. Outside, a fuzzy ray of sunshine reveals the blue light of dawn. I find a fountain pen and several sheets of paper. There are enough pages for me to write down my truth. It has to be longer than a will but shorter than an official report. I am running out of time but I may be able to finish it if I concentrate. After all, I'm not writing about my entire life, just about that one horrific moment in time. I press the pen on paper and the ink spreads like a bruise.

Dear Min-hwan, whom I have always respected and loved, I begin. The letter fills with script that looks like me—trying to look beautiful but nervous and wobbly and about to fall over. But I have to hold myself up and pull out the words so that I can leave something behind. It's terrible that this is all I can do for him. I write carefully, trying not to cry on the letter so the ink doesn't spread. My writing, as skinny as the bones of my arms and legs, smatters onto the white paper.

"Alice, what are you doing? We have to get going!" Hammett is busy with the reporters back at the barracks.

"How is she?"

Hammett takes my arm and pulls me aside. "She has a high fever again. I don't think she slept at all. I think we should cancel but she's insisting we continue. She really might come down with pneumonia if we keep to this schedule. And she has to go back to Tokyo tomorrow."

"Maybe the schedule was too ambitious for a bride on her honeymoon."

"Is she really a newlywed, anyway? Staying apart from her husband … I'll take care of the rest here. Go on to Seoul for the farewell reception."

I head to the airport. As I put the bags in the helicopter, an MP brings over a smaller bag. "This was in the truck."

Marilyn's makeup case. I thank him and get on the helicopter. A few others join me in the helicopter, looking tired: a couple of USO staff, a female singer with a fractured leg, a photographer. The last two days' bustle seems to have drained them of their vitality. I open my handbag to check on my letter. It still smells of ink. I take out the postcard Ku-yong drew for me before I left Seoul. Now I see that I look cross and pathetic in the picture. I let out a laugh. I don't want to admit it, but the flyer advertises his affection for me quite well. It brings him closer to his goal. He's such a talented artist. The war has ruined him, but he's trying to create again. Ku-yong's feelings towards me seem sincere, and perhaps if I'm honest I'm also interested in him, despite what I told him. Maybe I avoided getting involved because I was jealous; I was envious that he has managed to maintain a will and a passion for life. I think Ku-yong will recover. He might be the person who will mourn me the most when I'm gone from this world. Could it be that a man who hasn't even kissed me is the one who understands me best? Just like a book I haven't read could be a masterpiece that will bring me to tears.

Finally the helicopter gets ready for take-off. I never dreamed that Marilyn Monroe's blonde hair would be fluttering here, the Korean military's last line of defense, and I never imagined that I would be reunited here with the two most important men in my life. Who knows who they really are? I still can't believe they are both alive. They'll regret returning here and seeing me. The helicopter launches noisily with a swirl of dust. I lean against the window and look down. I'm lifted away from the ground. I imagine that life will feel as far away in the moment of death as the earth is now, and I'm suddenly afraid. But it might be better this way. If death is just a moment, like take-off, you would only have that moment for regrets.

I smell Seoul as soon as we land at Yoido Airport. The city isn't interested in someone who leaves and is even less interested when that person returns. Seoul doesn't expend energy by investing in someone's life. Although it was reduced to ash at each regime change, Seoul rose up quickly because it didn't expect much from humans. It always regains its pride on its own. I'm relieved that I'm safely back in Seoul, the perfect city in which to spend my last moments. I feel the wind in my hair as I send off my final farewell to Yu-ja and Mrs. Chang and Ku-yong. As I stand there in the dust kicked up by the wind, two black sedans race towards me and screech to a stop. Two agents, the same ones who questioned me two days ago, get out of the first one. Four Korean men emerge from the other car.

"Miss, can we talk in the car?" The agents aren't as coercive as last time, but they seem anxious.

I enter the car. The agents get in the front seats and the Korean driver sits next to me.

"Where's Joseph?" I ask.

"He's handling a personal matter. We're trying to reach him now," one of the agents explains. "We just learned that Lim Pok-hun is in Seoul. It seems he entered via an island off the western coast last week. We aren't sure if she's with him—"

I cut in. "Who? Seoul Crybaby?"

The agent sighs in irritation.

The driver quickly explains in Korean. "Yes. Without any proof that Lim has her under his protection, we can't put our men in danger and go along with the plan. He finally contacted someone on our side today, but this whole thing seems like a setup to ambush us. We need to be sure that it's not another Northern agent pretending to be him. You're the only one who knows what he looks like. Please, we need your help."

This is a significant wrench in my plan to kill myself today. "How could I possibly help?" I switch to Korean, too.

"We're supposed to meet him at Chungang Theater. We'd like you to be at the ticket booth to identify him. We won't put you in danger. We promise."

So it can get dangerous. Now my interest is piqued. "And if I don't cooperate?"

Their faces fall in unison. This might be my last official duty. I can already tell I have no choice in the matter.

"Okay. But are these two going to be there? They don't blend in." I point at the agents in the front seats. They look confused; they don't understand Korean. "Please give this to Joseph," I say to the agents in English, and take the letter out of my handbag. The white envelope is addressed to Yo Min-hwan.

I've only encountered Lim Pok-hun twice, but I've turned out to be a strong influence in his life. I am an undeniable goddess of misfortune. He eluded capture once. Now it seems he's found a way to escape his former masters. He's persistently lucky. What will happen when we meet again? I head to the theater to confirm our odd bond.

The first time I encountered Lim was at the Art Association offices in Chongno. One of my Tokyo art school classmates dragged me there. He never liked me; he introduced me to the others as a complete reactionary from a family that had sponged off the American military government for generations. I scoffed at them, never imagining that in due course, as corpses began rolling around the city center, they would try to reeducate me and force me to take up the brush for their purposes. They assigned me to the portrait division where I was to draw Stalin and Kim Il Sung from morning to night. My reward for offering my artistic talents and labor to the Party was a ball of cooked rice. Stalin was my closest friend during that terrible summer. I'd never drawn anyone's face as carefully as I did his—his jowly neck, his thick mustache, his flat eyes that had already transcended humanity. I never did like portraits or the sycophancy inherent in them. An artist poured all of her soul into a work; that meant that the subject of a portrait could only be the artist herself. I had secretly laughed at portrait subjects who were satisfied with their exaggeratedly perfect faces. That was how I drew Stalin's face, scoffing at him all the while. But he was grander than I expected, this politician who devoted himself to revolution. He shared his soul with the masses, attempting to stake a place for himself in the history books, conscientiously building his ambition. I devoted myself to his portraits despite myself, creating uniquely florid paintings.

One night in July, I was coloring Stalin's hair with quiet acrimony when someone spoke to me.

"Why are you drawing Comrade Stalin so ornately? He looks like an American movie star."

I raised my head and saw a stick-skinny man with a half-moon scar under one eye standing over me.

"Comrade Kim Ae-sun, I heard you were good. This, however, is a disappointment."

He already knew who I was. Having worked for the Americans, I was a target. I recognized him as a northern agent who sometimes stopped by the offices.

"Do you know where Yo Min-hwan is?" He spoke in smooth Seoul diction, though his enunciation was a little too careful.

"No," I replied feebly. "I haven't seen him in a long time." Why was he looking for Min-hwan, anyway? He wasn't that useful to the North, despite his time working for the Americans.

He stared at me and I didn't avoid his gaze, too depressed to even lie. He sneered and turned to leave. The pistol on his hip caught the light and glinted, glaring at me until he left the room.

The movie playing at Chungang Theater is an American film called *Unknown Island*. The man-eating dinosaur on the poster resembles a toy baring its teeth, no matter how generously I look at it. What kind of terror could this ridiculous monster unleash on humans? This is a silly movie for this postwar city, which has realized the immortal truth: man is the enemy of man. I enter the ticket booth, which reminds me of a prison visiting room. I'm relieved that I can't be seen from the outside, but that means I can't see out very well, either. A mirror is next to the ticket window to allow me to watch the customers while keeping the interior dark. The movie will start soon but not many people are lining up to buy tickets. The Korean agents are disguised as civilians and loitering in front of the theater, one dressed as a chestnut peddler and the other sweeping the sidewalk. They glance at me as people walk by. The ticking of the clock grows louder and louder. I am aware of every sound from the street. What if I don't recognize him after all?

It's ten to five and the movie theater is still mostly empty. A few couples, a group of women, and a few middle-aged men enter the theater. I count the seconds, looking at the clock anxiously. This mission is tilting towards failure. Maybe I should give up and go watch the movie myself.

I'm about to get up when a bony hand slides money in the ticket window.

"I would like one ticket, please." The man sounds proper and formal, as though he's reading from a textbook.

I take the money and glance at the mirror as I hand the ticket over. I pause, holding the change in my palm. He's wearing a dyed military cap and it's hard to see under the brim, but I detect a small, half-moon scar. It's him. I duck my head, waiting for him to leave. He moves away from the window but his footsteps boom in my ears as I put the "Sold Out" sign on the window with shaking hands. The agents see that and move quickly. The one disguised as a chestnut peddler yanks off his own hat and glances at his colleague. My part is done. Now I need to get to the car parked on the other side of the street. My legs are quaking. I come out of the ticket booth. I have to get out of here. But something holds me back. I'm curious. Finally, something real is going to happen in the theater. Genuine violence and flight, not just a story, directed and produced. Someone might die. A movie is just death made into art; the actors who kiss and dance onscreen are ghosts. They end up as particles of light in the darkened theater and vanish. I don't have any reason not to follow my instincts. I am the heroine of this movie. I am the one who knows the face of the enemy. I head to the dark hallway. I hear the thudding soundtrack of the movie. I push the heavy doors to go inside. I stop short; I can't see anything. The theater smells like mildew. I step forward cautiously. Then there's a crash.

"What's that?"

"Get him!"

"Over there!"

I turn my head and something dark smashes into me. I fall on the grimy floor. I hear running and get up quickly to chase after the footsteps. There is shouting and a clatter of feet outside the theater. I see someone dash away and I follow quietly. When I reach the end of the corridor, I don't see anyone. I'm about to turn around when I realize someone is standing behind me. I open my mouth to scream and a hand claps over it. I can't breathe. The cold, hard muzzle of a pistol digs into my back. He drags me to the back of the theater, his arm around my neck. He opens a door to the outside. It smells like oil paint. We are in the workshop where theater posters are painted; the space is covered by a makeshift tin roof stretching from the building to the wall. On the wall is a half-painted poster for an upcoming movie.

"It's been a long time, Kim Ae-sun," Lim says.

"I can slip you out of here," I say quickly.

Lim pushes me towards the wall. I bump into the poster and get blue paint on my shoulder. "What are you talking about?"

"I'm trying to help you."

"Why? You feel guilty for what you did on that ship?" Lim glances anxiously around, the gun still pointing at me.

"Why are you running away?"

He looks hounded, like a fleeing animal. I realize something: someone who holds all the cards would never be this nervous.

"Where is that woman?" I ask.

He wipes his forehead with the back of his hand holding the gun.

"She's dead, isn't she?" I surprise myself with my guess. But I think I'm right. "Seoul Crybaby isn't alive anymore, is she?"

Lim glares at me with a bitter half-smile.

"I'm right, aren't I? Did you kill her?"

"No. I really did try to help her."

"What happened?" I'm shaking.

"She was broken. She didn't even want to go back home. She just kept crying. I couldn't do anything. I needed her so I could get out."

"And?" *Please, please*, I think.

"She hanged herself." Lim's face darkens.

My hands fly up to my neck. This unknown woman's despair and sorrow spread through my body. I can imagine her clearly. She is beautiful and innocent, but everyone has the urge to debase an innocent woman. She is moaning, shedding tears, I can feel it all inside me. As I imagine her last moments I become infected with her grim courage. I hear rushing footsteps in the corridor. Lim grabs me by the throat. I don't know what he's planning to do with me, or how he means to escape this time, but I struggle. As I fall I grab the shelf to steady myself. Lim lunges to stop all the paint cans from falling, dropping the pistol and letting go of me.

I pick it up from the ground. I stand up.

"Give it here. It's not a toy." Lim's face is tense.

I realize I'm aiming the pistol at him. It's heavier and harder than I expected.

"Kim Ae-sun. Give it to me."

I stare at him. I'm possessed.

He looks more and more uncertain and horrified. "What are you doing?"

I turn the gun around slowly. The muzzle is now pointing at me. The gun isn't picky about who it wants to aim at. I grope at the trigger. It's surprisingly hard to find.

"Don't. I don't know what this is about, but you're going to make this worse for me than it already is." Lim is sweating. He inches forward as if approaching a wild beast.

I finally find the trigger. I slip my finger through with anticipation, as if I'm a bride sliding on her wedding ring.

"Alice!" Joseph is standing at the door.

I pull the trigger.

The gun goes off. There's a bang and then a sharp pain. I fall down. Darkness swoops over me. I hear more gunshots and footsteps.

"Are you okay?" It's Joseph.

The darkness pressing down on me lifts a little. Light begins to filter through.

Joseph picks up the poster that fell on top of me and helps me up. The agents are chasing after Lim. I try to look up but my head is too heavy. Something sticky is coursing down my scalp. It doesn't smell like blood—I know that smell all too well. I touch my head and my palm comes away stained yellow. The paint drips down the back of my neck. I'm an instant blonde. The bullet must have missed.

"What are you doing?" Joseph is holding me, looking teary. What an honor. This kind American intelligence officer is about to shed tears for me. "And what did you mean by that letter?"

I smile at him.

He shakes me hard, angrily. "What is going on? Alice! Get a hold of yourself!"

"Where's Min-hwan?"

"Looking for his daughter. When he went to the orphanage he discovered it wasn't her. It was Chong-nim."

"What? You found her?" My heart starts to pound.

"No. I'm sorry. Chong-nim had been moved to a different orphanage. She was gone by the time we got there. It's clear she's not his daughter. But why would she have his watch? He was certain it was Song-ha because of that watch."

Everything turns fuzzy. Joseph's face doubles and overlaps with itself. It feels like blood and oil are gushing out of every pore of my being. My legs shake. I think I'm going to vomit. Every time Joseph tries to get me up, yellow paint gets on his shoulder.

"I'm sorry. He'll never find his daughter. I killed her."

"You're not in your right mind," Joseph says, shaking his head. "You haven't been in a long time."

I'm not sure myself if what I'm saying is really true. But I know it's highly likely. Because the truth tends to be what people don't want to believe is true.

Dear Min-hwan, whom I have always respected and loved,

I think I'm still dreaming. I can't believe I fell asleep in your arms last night. You vanished from my life years ago. It's been difficult. It was hard to even utter your name. After I heard you were purged, I couldn't sleep. I was afraid your soul would come back, that your ghost would haunt me. But a part of me was relieved that you died. I'm sorry to say this but I was glad I didn't have to see you again in this lifetime. Of course, all of that doesn't matter anymore. I won't be able to escape you now. You'll probably want to go back to how things were, when we were in love and were bound up, however painfully, in each other's lives. But we can't. It was a miracle that I saw you again, but I can't bring myself to face you, and that's why I'm writing to you. All of this, all of your tragedies, began with a damn letter, so it's only fitting that we end it this way.

Joseph and I humiliated and betrayed you. You say you want to forget about all of that but you shouldn't. That is the kind of thing that can't ever be forgotten. I think our lives are influenced by truly unforgettable events. I think I did it because I sensed we were going our separate ways. I couldn't stand it, so I simply lost my mind for a moment. That's probably when the insanity inside of me began to emerge. I thought I was going to suffocate when you refused to see me. I wrote that letter out of a foolish sense of revenge. I wanted to shock your wife and create divisions in your family. That was all. So I wrote to her saying that we wanted to officially get married and that we should negotiate the terms. It was a stupid, terrible, mean thing to do. I never imagined it would bring your wife to see me.

You said that after the war broke out you went to find your wife at her parents' home but she wasn't there. That's because she was in Seoul.

My uncle and his family left the city as soon as the war began. The wealthy Koreans reassured the other citizens and exhorted them to protect the city, but then they left on their own private trains. My uncle wanted me to come along but I insisted on staying. I had to wait for you. If you decided to forgive me, if you said you would go north with me, I would have gone. But I couldn't find you and the war was growing more serious than I expected. Seoul fell in a mere three days to the People's Army and the Han River bridge was bombed. We were isolated. We couldn't withdraw any money because the presidential emergency order froze all bank accounts. Who knew where they had been hiding, but boys ran out into the streets, shouting, "Hooray for General Kim Il Sung!" I was home alone, growing worried and flustered, when someone knocked on the front gates. It was a lady in a beautiful blue hanbok holding the hand of an adorable girl wearing a navy blue sailor dress. Your wife and your beloved daughter Song-ha.

Your wife possessed a noble, elegant disposition. I could tell right away. She wiped her brow with a white handkerchief and explained that she had received my letter. I stood frozen in place as she told me calmly that she had decided she would settle this matter once and for all and got on a train to Seoul. She didn't tell anyone her plans—she wanted to protect your dignity and her pride. She brought Song-ha, hoping she could appeal to my humanity. But as soon as she arrived at Seoul Station, she faced hordes of people fleeing the city. She rushed to your place but you weren't there; even the owner of your boarding house had left. She waited for a while in that empty house before coming to see me.

In a melodrama, the wife and the mistress would fight, but we didn't have even that luxury. I'd searched for you everywhere but had no idea where you were. I had to invite her to stay with me. She didn't know anyone else in Seoul. And she had run out of money. She declined over and over again but there was no other solution. We started living together, as wife and as concubine. Every day, we sat together listening intently to the radio for news. The militia came and took all of our rice and claimed the house as their office. We were relegated to a corner room upstairs. When I complained, a young man politely apologized, but it was clear that the liberation they were carrying out wouldn't protect us. We had to try to leave Seoul. I had heard you could hire someone to row you across the river from Mapo or Sogang. We fled, taking turns carrying Song-ha on our backs, but bombs rained down on us and we had to turn around before we even reached Ahyon-dong. The rotting corpses piled in the streets were a problem, but hunger was an even bigger issue. I had been taken to the Art Association and was assigned to draw portraits of Stalin there every day, but at least it meant I could bring back some barley. Your wife carried Song-ha on her back and made meals for the militia. She was a good woman. She was dignified, even when she had to live under the same roof as her husband's mistress, unable to leave because of the war. She pretended not to notice as I scurried about, flustered and guilty, wondering what she was thinking. We suffered through that ridiculous situation without speaking. One day, I came home late after a long day at the Association.

*She told me to take off my soiled blouse so she could wash it for
me. I snapped at her, telling her it was fine and she should stop.
Her face remained composed as she said she didn't consider me
her husband's mistress, but as a nobody, and that it helped her
live through this time. I asked her how she was able to do that,
and she said it came from years of an unhappy marriage. To
protect herself from unhappiness, she chose not to see it. I was
stunned. I always thought of her as a pitiful, sad woman, but in
reality she was strong, much stronger than me. She was spending
lonely, uneasy days with me, protecting herself from grief in her
own way. And the source of that strength was Song-ha. She was
quiet and lovable, just like you. I tried to avoid her out of guilt
and jealousy, but ended up completely charmed by her. She was
darling, she was smart, and she was impressive, trying not to cry
when bombs began dropping. When I asked her, "How much do
you like your father?" she would primly turn away and take out
your pocket watch to show me. I can't forget that pale, plump
face. We survived thanks to that dear girl. Around August,
Song-ha fell sick. It could have been malnutrition—there was a
severe food shortage. Our next-door neighbor went to get food
from a farm in Kyonggi Province but he got caught in a
bombing campaign and his legs were blown off, though he
managed to survive. I sliced the belly of Song-ha's stuffed bear
and shook out the stuffing—millet—to make porridge. Your
wife fell ill from overwork. The People's Committee trampled
through the house for what they called training and ended up
burning part of it down. In the middle of the night, I snuck
outside and dug up a piece of gold my relatives had buried before
they fled. I sold it on the black market and bought canned food.*

I went to Dr. Han Mi-ja, who lost all three sons to the militia and was guarding the empty Seoul Clinic by herself. Thankfully, when I explained that they were your family, she welcomed them. We spent each day terrified as flyers fell from the sky, announcing that Seoul would soon be bombed and we should leave. I was tormented by your family's suffering. It was all because of my mischief. If you came back to me, I vowed, I would send you back to them. I would return you to where you should have been all along. Thankfully Song-ha got better. Your wife also felt energized after a few days' rest in the clinic. That cruel summer was beginning to wane. It was September; the war would soon be decided one way or another.

We followed the movements of the UN forces by clandestinely listening to a shortwave radio. Seoul continued to be bombed. A rumor circulated that if the South Korean army took control of Seoul again, people who had worked for the northern regime would be targeted. In any case, we waited for you to find us. The bombings grew more forceful and we heard that the UN forces had landed in Inchon. The People's Army became more desperate. After Chusok, everyone was wondering and whispering about the state of the war. Battles began erupting in the streets. We heard that public figures were tied together and dragged up north through the hills of Miari. People were getting slaughtered. We were told that in the countryside, Americans, supposedly on our side, had shoved civilians in a tunnel and killed them all, including the children.

On September 22, rumor had it that American soldiers were spotted near Yongdungpo. I hurried home in the middle of cleaning up in the office. The yard usually bustled with military exercises but it was empty that day. *My heart pounded with a strange premonition. I ran to the Seoul Clinic, worried about your wife and Song-ha. I had just turned down the alley towards the clinic when I heard gunfire. I sank to the ground; a woman was crying, running towards me in stockinged feet, screaming, "She's gone crazy, she's gone crazy! Dr. Han attacked the soldiers with a kitchen knife, screaming to bring her sons back ..." I staggered to my feet and ran into the yard, shaking. It smelled like gunpowder. Dust was flying. People were lying under the ginkgo tree. Even though I saw blood seeping through their clothes I didn't realize they were dead. There was more gunfire. People's Army soldiers were pointing guns at a dozen people standing before them. They were shooting each of them, as if doing target practice, without even the consideration of blindfolding them. A woman with a baby on her back tried to flee, but slumped over after a loud bang. I rubbed my eyes hard and looked carefully. Terrified sobs echoed in my ears. I spotted your wife at the end of the line, hugging Song-ha tightly, her back turned towards the soldiers. I cried out and she looked up. She didn't have any fear in her eyes, only love. She was holding Song-ha ever tighter, to give that young life as much love as she possibly could to the very end. I ran forward, screaming. Your wife pushed Song-ha, who was crying and clinging to her, towards me. Gunfire. Your wife blocked the bullets with her thin back and collapsed. I struggled to pull Song-ha out from under her. There was more gunfire. I felt a sharp pain in my side and lost consciousness.*

I opened my eyes. It was dark and everything smelled of blood. I must be in hell, *I thought. I couldn't move. It was as if I had sunk into a swamp. When I finally managed to move my*

150

head and looked around, I had to bite down on my tongue so as not to scream. The squishy, heavy swamp was made up of bodies. Above my head was the sky, blue and round. I was near the top of a pile of corpses, thrown into a dry well. I wasn't dead. I pushed against the bodies and pulled my upper body out with all my might. Below me was a boy in a school uniform and an old man. Between them was Song-ha. I grabbed her by the arm and pulled her out. Her blue sailor dress was soaked in blood but I saw her eyebrows squirm. She let out a deep breath. I heard men above. They hadn't left yet. I put a hand against her mouth and curled around her. I trained my ears to the outside. They were walking around the well. I felt Song-ha's wet breath against my palm. She was alive. I kept still until it became quiet, my head against someone's bloodied, torn-up behind. I stayed like that for a long time. When I looked up again the sky was purple. I couldn't hear anything outside. I tried to step on the tangle of corpses to climb up. I couldn't stand. I kept slipping. I shook Song-ha. "Song-ha," I said. She didn't wake up. I looked down at my palm where I'd felt her breath. She had vomited a clump of blood. "No, Song-ha, open your eyes. You're just sleeping. Wake up. It's morning." I kept shaking her. I started to scream for help. "Help, we're alive in here!" My voice circled the well, unable to break out. I tried to climb up with her in my arms but I couldn't make any progress. I kept shouting and crying. The corpses beneath my feet began rising up and saying, "You're the only one who survived. You're the only one." Their laughter began spreading outside the well. "Shut up," I shouted. I put my hands over Song-ha's ears so she couldn't hear them. She was getting colder. I took my blouse off and draped it over her. A warm corpse, whose head was leaning against my ankle, whispered, snickering, "What's the point of surviving?" All the ghosts agreed and laughed at me. I called for help all night long. I lost consciousness near dawn, watching the lights of a jet descending like a falling star. The next day neighbors hauled me out of the well. When I emerged with Song-ha on my back, people stared at me, their mouths hanging open. Overnight my hair had turned entirely gray. My nails were all broken. I was drenched in the blood of dead strangers. I put my hands to my mouth, then began to strangle myself until I fainted. I was holding Song-ha's pocket watch in my hand.

That's what really happened. Now I wash my hair with Crown beer, because it never recovered its color. Everything else changed. I spent each day in the camps, on the wharf in Hungnam, in Pusan as a refugee, with the awareness that only I had survived from that well. People called me insane but I couldn't even truly go crazy. I just trembled when there were too many people. I tried to kill myself but that was just a shrewd ploy; I didn't have the courage to actually go through with it. I would have continued to live meaninglessly in this way if I hadn't seen you again. But yesterday, when I was with you, I realized that people find ways to continue on despite their pain. You still had hope, not realizing that it was baseless. I have wrestled with whether to keep this secret to myself, but I decided to come clean for you, for me, for your wife and Song-ha. I don't think I can continue on with this by myself. I think it's time. Death won't save me, but maybe it can spare your life.

I can no longer imagine how life could be beautiful. I just pass the time surviving, without living. I don't have any *attachment to this life, and I won't dare hope for your forgiveness. I'm just satisfied that I saw you again. You loved me when I was at my most beautiful. Without seeing you again, I wouldn't have remembered that I was once cherished. I knew love and felt happiness at one point. Thank you for that. What would have happened if there hadn't been a war? Would we still be together? It's not all because of the war, of course. They say the war was the greatest tragedy of our era, borne from ideological conflict. But, for me, war was the thing that caused me to kill the child of the man I loved. Min-hwan, please don't ruin your future by hating me. Please don't pity me. I couldn't vanquish the war inside of me, and in the end I lost. I wish you a very happy life. I have found my last duty. I'm ready. I feel at peace with my decision.*

Joseph glares at me with exasperation. "It was a tragic accident. You didn't kill his daughter!"

"I could have kept her alive. She was alive when I found her." I sound vacant even to myself.

"That's nonsense. You're just feeling guilty. What's the point of bringing that up right now?" Joseph shakes me. I've never seen him this angry.

"They wouldn't have come to Seoul if I hadn't sent that letter. It's my fault."

Joseph rips the letter out of his pocket and waves it violently in the air. "Are you trying to martyr yourself for that?"

"I'm the one who ruined their lives. I have to pay for it."

"And what precisely will change if you die?"

"At least I don't have to face him." I feel nauseated. I grip my chest and vomit. Thick green stuff spills out of my mouth.

Joseph looks down at me quietly, his pretty tea-colored eyes cold. "Do you still not understand what kind of man he is? Betrayal is a two-way street. It's just that each person finds out at different times." He kneels and picks the gun off the ground. "Like you said, I knew the war was imminent. So did Min-hwan. I can't tell you how he knew, but I can tell you that he loved his family more than he loved you. He asked me to help take his wife and daughter to safety. He disappeared so suddenly because he was supposed to go to Japan with them. But his wife had left her parents' house before I could get to her. They were fated to miss each other. Do you get it now? He left you first." Joseph brushes his knees as he stands up.

The other agents return and report that they lost Lim. "He ran out the back before we could catch him. Now we've lost Seoul Crybaby, too."

"That woman?" I ask. It seems Lim's luck has held once more. "Don't look for her." Her famously weepy voice shakes my soul and grows louder. I speak on her behalf. "She doesn't want to come back. Ever. Not to Seoul—not to goddamn Seoul."

Luxury cars are lining up in front of the Bando Hotel. Foreigners, women in fur coats and gowns and men in tails, are entering in pairs as if waltzing.

"Will you be okay, Alice?" Joseph sounds worried. "Go wash up and rest. You may have to cut your hair and use something strong to get the paint off. Here, give me your scarf." He takes my scarf off my neck and puts it over my head.

I look at my reflection in the car window. Bright yellow hair pokes out from under the scarf. It's funny and terrifying at the same time. I kiss him on the cheek. "Good night. Let's talk tomorrow."

"Alice," Joseph calls as I'm about to get out of the car.

"Go finish your assignment. I have to clean this up." I point at my hair and smile.

Joseph nods sorrowfully. "Okay. Sweet dreams."

I watch Joseph's car get smaller in the darkness, then go into the hotel. It's crammed with excited people hoping to attend Marilyn Monroe's farewell reception. I find a newspaper next to an ashtray and hide behind the paper as I step into the elevator. It lifts up into the air with a baritone groan. I'm riveted by the article in front of my nose, reading it over and over again. A maid has killed her employer's children. The young maid had been raped by her employer and, after miscarrying the baby, she had pushed his children over a ravine to their deaths. The maid explained calmly that she was glad. I remember the raging, despairing girl I had seen hunched in the cold corridor of the clinic. The world hadn't granted her any kindness or peace. It weighs heavily on me. I'm not sure I can stand straight. The elevator stops and holds me still but I'm already free-falling into the girl's deep, troubled eyes.

Thankfully I make it to the room without encountering anyone. Open suitcases are strewn about near the bed. I stagger towards the vanity. Marilyn's makeup bag is wide open. I sit down and take the scarf off my head.

I'm looking at a blonde Alice. The yellow paint is drying, crusted on my hair, and it smells awful. It has covered nearly all of my head. My blondness isn't fatally seductive; it's slightly sad. I look like an actress now; I decide that I will act the part of a woman who is betrayed by a man and chooses a tragic end.

I rummage through the bag for lipstick. I find a tangle of perfume and makeup and high-end brushes made of weasel fur. I take out a red lipstick and smear it on crookedly. It's bold and beautiful. But now I don't like how my face looks. I find two boxes of Coty powder. One is the real thing and the other, as I expected, is filled with phenobarbital pills.

I take them out and move to the bed. The small messengers of death are snug in my palm. They'll coast through my bloodstream, singing and dancing all night long, until I fall asleep. Around their last dance, my soul will say goodbye to my body. I spot a glass of whiskey next to the bed. I drink some down. My mouth is on fire. I bring the pills to my lips.

"Alice?"

I flinch and drop the pills, and they thud onto the floor like bullets. I turn around. Marilyn is standing right behind me, looking surprised. Our mouths hang open as we stare at one other.

I recover quickly. "Oh, I'm sorry. I was trying to clean up but I made more of a mess." I kneel on the floor, trying to hide my flustered state, and pick up the pills.

Marilyn hurries to bend over and help. Hunching over in her sparkling white dress, she looks like a pretty trumpet-shaped shell. She keeps stealing glances at me.

I put the pills back into the sweet-smelling Coty box.

"And your hair!" Marilyn exclaims.

"What do you think? Do you think I look a little more like you?"

She tugs at me and drags me to the mirror. It looks like I'm wearing a broom. Or maybe the sun. Marilyn opens her mouth and closes it, studying me quizzically, before bursting into a gale of laughter.

I laugh along awkwardly. Now we're both holding our bellies.

She loops her arm through mine. "Well, here we are, two fake blondes." She smiles as she picks the yellow paint flecks off my shoulder.

Suddenly I feel a tingle on the tip of my nose. I burst into tears. Marilyn stares at me in shock as I laugh and cry.

I shouldn't frighten our treasured guest. I try to explain. "It's okay," I tell her. "It's nothing. I had an accident. It was because of a man."

Her clear eyes sparkle. "Oh, no. A man causing trouble again?"

I laugh, disarmed by the girlish expression on her face, unbefitting her generous chest. "Yes, as usual. Today was really tough. Do you have days like that, when you're fed up because of a man? When you feel so lonely? I thought maybe I wouldn't be able to fall asleep without some pills, but now, thanks to you, I think I'll be able to. Thank you, Marilyn." I pull her into a hug. She's befuddled.

She has rescued me from my despair. Having betrayed the man I loved and having been betrayed by him, I was about to succumb to a misfortune of my own making. I am honored that the person who saved me is the most beautiful woman in the world. Somehow, tonight, beauty is what ends up saving my life.

Goodbye, Blondes!

February 19, 1954

THE FANS ARE DOWNCAST, GATHERED AT YOIDO AIRPORT to see Marilyn off. There are fewer of them than when she arrived but it's still a large crowd. A soldier is crying, clutching a present he wants to give her. Her car pulls in and everyone rushes over.

Marilyn gets out and hugs the high-level officials. Someone taps me on the shoulder. It's Joseph, his coat collar popped up. He beckons for me to come with him. He climbs into one of the four-engine fighters going to Tokyo. I follow him. Min-hwan is waiting there. He stands up when he sees me. He is wearing horn-rimmed glasses and a hat, still in half-hearted disguise. "We didn't find her," he tells me, looking anxious.

"I heard." I glance at Joseph, who nods as if he knows nothing.

"I have to get back to Tokyo," Min-hwan says. "You'll come with me, won't you?"

"I'm going to stay."

He squints at me as I stand in the doorway. His expression catches at my heart.

"Why? What's here for you?"

"I have someone I have to find, too."

Min-hwan's shoulders sink and he lets out a sigh. "Are you sure?"

I look him squarely in the face. It's taking all my courage, but I know I need to let him go. "Have a nice trip."

"Next time, then. Let's go back together."

I offer him my brightest smile. "Bye."

Min-hwan is mute with disappointment.

I scramble off. I'm glad he doesn't come out after me.

"You're really going to stay?" Joseph asks with concern from the top of the stairs.

"Come back when my hair turns black again. And will you burn that letter for me?"

Joseph nods gravely.

I trust that he will do it. I turn around decisively. I will wait bravely for Min-hwan's revenge or for my fate to catch up with me. I sheathe the memory of my wrongdoing and hone my fighting spirit. This is what I need to do for myself as I embark on my battle. I cannot forget for a moment that my own war—Chong-nim's war—hasn't come to an end. I go back to the crowd surrounding Marilyn. People are unable to let her go. Finally, it's my turn. She gives me a warm hug. The wind tugs my scarf off my hair. My yellow-painted hair is revealed under the sun. She smiles at me. I hand her a small package.

"What's this?"

"A little souvenir. Open it when you get home." It's a portrait of Marilyn. Watching the lines of her beautiful face come alive under my hand had given me a spark of joy I haven't felt in a long time. "Oh, and a friend of mine wanted me to wish you congratulations on your marriage."

"Thank you. It has been wonderful. I'll never forget Korea. Oh, Alice—I don't even know your Korean name."

"You would need to practice for a whole year to pronounce it correctly."

Marilyn laughs.

"Just remember me as Alice J. Kim."

"J? What does it stand for?" Marilyn's brows arch like seagulls, puzzled.

"June," I say. "The month I was born and the month the war began. I gave it to myself."

Author's Note

THIS BOOK WAS INSPIRED BY TWO PHOTOGRAPHS.

One was of a female interpreter at work, standing between a UN soldier and a North Korean POW during the Korean War, and the other was of Marilyn Monroe, who visited Korea right after the war to perform for the American military.

I had the same question when I saw these two pictures, both against the backdrop of the Korean War but so very different from each other.

Where did all the beautiful and hopeful young women go?

I always thought it strange that my parents' generation, having lived through the Korean War (1950–53), rarely talked about it. The Korean War, also known as the Forgotten War, is far in the past now, with fewer survivors remaining every year. As I gathered war recollections and experiences, it occurred to me that oblivion might have been critical for survival. All of the stories I heard were terrible and unjust and tragic. It made me think it would be better to forget.

In Kurt Vonnegut's *Slaughterhouse-Five*, the main character says he wants to write an anti-war novel. A movie maker says he should write an anti-glacier book instead. I'm sure that for someone like me, who didn't experience war first-hand, writing about it isn't all that different from touching only the tip of an enormous glacier. But I couldn't tear my eyes away from these two women in the photographs. They captivated me. I wanted to tell their stories. How did a woman who had a tragic life arm herself in a tragic era? Everyone has at least one weapon with which they protect their own lives, something that makes you stand your ground in the face of atrocity and violence.

In February 1954, Marilyn Monroe came to Korea to perform for American soldiers stationed here. Wearing a slinky dress on a makeshift stage, she sang "Diamonds Are a Girl's Best Friend" as it snowed. Ten thousand American marines went wild. Later, Monroe would look back at that performance and say that it was the first time in her life she felt like a real star. For her, Korea was an unforgettable place.

Every time I looked at the picture of Monroe, I was taken by it. It's surreal to see the most famous bombshell of the day singing on top of rubble. At the same time, she was surprisingly approachable. This wasn't something allowed only to Marilyn Monroe, I realized. All women who survived war had the right to revel in being alive, dancing and singing like Marilyn. It made me understand the women who frequented the dance halls in postwar Korea, which was a hotly debated issue at the time. Maybe they were emitting light and embracing life because they had experienced death. I wanted to write about the women who struggled to come alive. Marilyn Monroe herself had to change to become a goddess. I think she was the victim of her own beauty. If I could meet her, I would ask her if she could have been stronger, more vicious, more solitary so that she wouldn't have had to sacrifice herself. Like our friend Alice J. Kim.

Though Alice and the other characters in the story could have lived in the era depicted here, they are fictional. The book is based on real events but enhanced with my imagination. I hope readers will be generous at my attempt to reveal more of the glacier. This book is deeply indebted to those who survived and those who didn't. My sincere thanks to Yun Il-gyun and Mun Chang-jae, who allowed me to incorporate events described in their books. I am grateful to the many people who helped in the writing of this book, as well as everyone at That Book publishing company, who truly cared for this project. Thank you to my parents and my family, especially to my son and husband, who were so understanding while I wrote. As it happens, I'm writing this note on June 25, the day the Korean War began. The gravity of the day will always be in my heart.

References

Harimao T. Musashiya, *38seondo 6.25 hankuk jeonjaengdo migukui jakpumieotda* [The 38th Parallel and the Korean War, Product of the USA] (Seoul: Saeroun Saramdeul, 1998).

Hughes, Dudley, *Wall of Fire: A Diary of the Third Korean Winter Campaign* (Central Point, OR: Hellgate Press, 2003). Translated from the English by Im In-chang (Seoul: *Korea Economic Daily, 2008*).

Jeong Il-hwa, *Aneun geotgwa dareun maekadeoui hanguk jeonjaeng* [What You Didn't Know About MacArthur's Korean War] (Seoul: Mirae Hankuk Sinmun, 2007).

Kim Seong-chil, *Yeoksa apeseo—han sahakjaui 6.25 ilgi* [In Front of History: One Historian's Korean War Diary] (Paju: Changbi, 1997).

Kim Seong-hwan, *Gobau gimseonghwanui panjachon iyagi* [Life in the Shantytown] (Paju: Yeollimwon, 2005).

Kim Won-il, et al., *Nareul ullin hangukjeonjaeng 100 jangmyeon* [One Hundred Scenes of the Korean War That Made Me Cry], translated by Park Do (Seoul: Nunbit, 2006).

Ko Gil-seop, *21 tongui yeoksa jinjeongseo* [Representation of History through Twenty-One Letters] (Seoul: Elpi, 2005).

Korea National University of Arts and Korea National Research Center for the Arts, eds., *Korean Contemporary Art History Series 1* (Seoul: Sigong Art, 1999).

Arthur W. Wilson, Korean Vignettes: Faces of War (Artwork Pbns, 1996). Translated from the English by Kim Nam-hyong (Seoul: Baekam, 2008)

Korea Psychology Research Institute, ed., *Naega gyeokeun haebanggwa bundan* [My Experience Living through Korea's Liberation and Division] (Seoul: Seonin, 2001).

Ko Un, *1950nyeondae—geu pyeheoui munhakgwa ingan* [1950s: The Literature and Humanity of the Ruins] (Seoul: Hyangyeon, 2005).

Lee Hyeon-hui, *Naega gyeokeun 6.25 jeonjaeng haui seoul 90il* [My Ninety Days in Seoul During the Korean War] (Busan: Hyomin, 2008).

Lee Im-ha, *Yeoeong, jeonjaengeul neomeo ileoseoda* [Women Rising Beyond War] (Seoul: Seohae Munjib, 2007).

Lee Yun-gyu, *Deulliji anteon chongseong joingipoktan!—6.25jeonjaenggwa simrijeon* [Paper Bombs, the Silent

Gunfire: The Korean War and Psychological Warfare]
(Seoul: Seongrim, 2006).

Monroe, Marilyn, *My Story* (New York: Stein and Day,
1974). Translated from the English by Lee Hyeon-
jong (Seoul: Haenaem, 2003).

Mun Chang-jae, ed., *Jeonjangui hayan chonesadeul—Jo
Gwirye hoigorok* [White Angels of the Battlefield: The
Memoirs of Cho Gwi-rye] (Seoul: Hankook
Munhwasa, 2007).

Rollyson, Carl, *Marilyn Monroe: A Life of the Actress*, rev.
ed. (Jackson: University of Mississippi Press, 2004).
Translated from the English by Lee Ji-seon (Seoul:
Yedam, 2003)

Yun Il-gyun, *Hanmi hapdong cheopbo bihwa 6006budae*
[Behind the Scenes of Korean-US Intelligence Unit
6006] (Paju: Korean Studies Information, 2006).